VOYAGE ALONG
THE HORIZON

VOYAGE ALONG THE HORIZON

by JAVIER MARÍAS

TRANSLATED FROM THE SPANISH
by KRISTINA CORDERO

BELIEVER BOOKS

a tiny division of

MCSWEENEY'S
which is also small

BELIEVER BOOKS
a division of
McSWEENEY'S

826 Valencia Street
San Francisco, CA 94110

© 1972 Javier Marías
Translation by Kristina Cordero

books.believermag.com

Cover design by Alvaro Villanueva.
Cover illustration by Jonathon Rosen.

Printed in Canada by Westcan Printing Group.

ISBN: 1-932-41618-8

CONTENTS

BOOK ONE 9

BOOK TWO 13

BOOK THREE 43

BOOK FOUR 69

BOOK FIVE 99

BOOK SIX 141

BOOK SEVEN 161

BOOK EIGHT 171

APPENDIX: EIGHT QUESTIONS FOR JAVIER MARÍAS 175

BOOK ONE

Even now, I cannot be sure whether his intentions were purely romantic—as he reiterated far too often—or if his many strategies were in fact a belated attempt to re-establish his somewhat faded reputation as an intrepid adventurer; or if they were a response to the shameless offers of some or other scientific institution, though I sincerely doubt that was the case. What I can say, however, is that those of us who found ourselves entangled in this allowed ourselves to be seduced by his passion and persistence, and I would even go so far as to say—though it pains me to say so given what happened in the end—that when the first few obstacles began to materialize when we were still on dry land, and there was talk of abandoning something that was still a mere proposition, it was our little coterie—and not the oppor-tunistic men of science whose influence with the authorities had secured them a place on the trip—that was the most determined to overcome these problems and set sail, despite the adversities and the very abominable conditions under which we would do so.

Perhaps it is not very honest of me to say so, and perhaps I am only trying to console myself with false conclusions, but I do think that under other circumstances—in Paris, for example—things would have unfolded in a very different manner indeed. Had we first met on the Boulevard des Italiens some spring morning or at the opera, during a delectable intermission in Mme D'Almeida's box, instead of the middle of those vast, nauseating waters that surrounded us on all sides, day in and day out, it is entirely possible that the grievances I now harbor would be expressed with a bit more savoir-faire and a bit less bile.

In Alexandria, the climate is quite unpredictable from December to March, though in general the days are sunny and cold, and only on the odd occasion is the city battered by heavy precipitation, sleet, and thunderous wind. August is the balmiest month, and though the sea breeze does alleviate the high temperatures at this time of year, the humidity is considerable and, I might add, quite bad for the health. The city, known as Al Iskandariyah to its inhabitants, is located on a strip of land that separates the Mediterranean from Lake Mareotis, a T-shaped promontory dotted with ports to the east and west alike. Long ago, the vertical arm of the T was a landmass that stretched all the way out to the island of Pharos, the eastern edge of which was outfitted with a lighthouse under the orders of Ptolemy II, for the exorbitant price of 800 talents. The prettiest part of the city may well be the port; if not, it would have to be the Grand Square (formerly known as the Place des Consuls), the northern face of which is graced by the Anglican Church of St. Mark, which sits atop a piece of land that Mohammed Ali the Great bequeathed to the British Community here in 1839. It is without a doubt the most European part of the city.

The feeling that you have made a fool of yourself, that you have wasted an opportunity you have sought for so long, that you have acted dishonorably, forever ruined a very well laid plan, failed to rise to the occasion, lacked tact and self-control, seemed impertinent and unpleasantly obvious, lost someone's respect—in short, the feeling that you have behaved like a perfect lout, is perhaps one of the most painful and humiliating sensations a man can ever know.

A few hours later, however, when I reexamined all the facts of the story, as the light evening breeze cleared and calmed my mind, I felt my chagrin alleviated and my serenity restored. You see, I am a man who tends to be acquiescent and easy to please, and when people like myself abandon an endeavor or illusion we usually have little trouble finding the right arguments to convince us that our plans were in fact quite insipid; these arguments, in turn, allow us to actually feel thrilled and relieved when our endeavor goes awry. And so, the following morning, everything—or at least near-ly everything—had already been forgotten.

BOOK TWO

Upon hearing the name of a man who, according to one of the other guests, had enjoyed a lofty position in society for many years until he died penniless as the result of his excessive love for painting, the gentleman before me—whose name I hadn't quite caught when he had been introduced to me two hours earlier—grimly acknowledged the chillingly similar and recent demise of a good friend of his, a man who had spent both his life and his fortune trying to discover the reasons for which Victor Arledge, at the beginning of his so-called "golden years," abandoned literature and locked himself away in a distant relative's mansion in Scotland, where he died three years later at the age of thirty-eight. After some very intense questioning by a woman who, I later learned, had written a thesis about the famous author but knew nothing of the existence or the literary investigations of this second unfortunate soul, the gentleman before me, Mr. Holden Branshaw (or Hordern Bragshawe, I cannot be certain), responded that although his friend had been unable to fully establish the complete set of causes that had led to the demise of such an accomplished writer as Victor Arledge, his friend had indeed succeeded in gathering enough information to cobble together an ambiguous, intriguing story about the writer in question. According to Mr. Branshaw—or was it Bragshawe?—his friend had spent the final year of his life weaving all this information together into a novel that he entitled *Voyage Along the Horizon,* and Mr. Branshaw, who had this novel in his possession, firmly believed that once it was published, his friend would finally be recognized as one of the great novelists of his time, which would prove that though this endeavor may have cost him both his fortune and his life, at the very least it had not been a waste of his time.

Mr. Branshaw's categorical affirmations to this effect elicited no reaction whatsoever from any of the people standing with him, and after about another half an hour, as the evening began to wane and the gathering fell into a bit of a lull, the guests all rose in unison—such a like-minded group, down to the tiniest detail— and bid me goodbye, though not without thanking me profusely for inviting them to enjoy such a pleasant evening at my home. And they left. When I returned to the salon, I saw that neither Mr. Branshaw nor the lady who had written her thesis on Victor Arledge had moved from their chairs, and were now chatting away with tentative but quite genuine enthusiasm. After pouring myself a glass of port, making as little noise as possible so as not to disturb them, I sat down in an easy chair. The rather petite lady, whose age was as elusive to me as the color of her simple dress and the reason for her presence in my living room, continued questioning Mr. Branshaw about his friend's novel with courteous if rather poorly concealed excitement, and at the end of this subtle battle in which Branshaw clearly held the upper hand (his replies to all her questions were laconic even though it was obvious she was terribly eager to hear them), the lady finally ventured to ask him if she might borrow the novel for a few days, given that its publication would remain uncertain until Arledge's family decided whether or not to permit the revelation of so many secrets regarding the author's life and times. To my surprise—perhaps it was the lady's aforementioned insistence, coupled with the gentleman's very obvious attempts to momentarily stave off her questions—he suggested they meet again, and they made arrangements to see one another the following morning at Holden Branshaw's home, where he would read the book aloud to the lady, because he did not wish to part with the original copy of the manuscript, not even for a few days. And I have no idea why—perhaps he was just being polite, or perhaps he was simply terrified by the thought of having to be alone with the lady—but without missing a beat Branshaw then turned to me and insisted I join them at his house the next day if I found the topic compelling or even mildly interesting. Out of simple courtesy, I replied that I wouldn't dream of missing the reading and thanked him for the kind invitation. Following this, Holden Branshaw and the petite lady, her face aglow with satisfaction, said their goodbyes, left my house, and went off in the directions of their respective homes.

I woke up the following day—later than normal and somewhat addled by my last glass of port the night before, having completely forgotten about Mr. Branshaw—to the sound of a chambermaid violently banging at my door, with the very pressing announcement that a Miss Bunnage had been waiting for me in the sitting room for some ten minutes. For a moment or two I idly wondered who on earth she was talking about, and then hastened to wash and dress without lingering any more over the identity of this person who—I might as well say it—had had the nerve to show up at my house unannounced at nine-thirty in the morning. In less-than-ideal spirits I finally made my way downstairs and, before I even set foot in the sitting room, the lady from the previous evening jumped up to greet me, bubbling over with eager anticipation.

"Please excuse the unexpected visit," she said. "But I was on my way to Mr. Branshaw's house and as I passed by I thought I might offer you a ride there. My carriage is waiting outside, and we're already running late."

I couldn't remember the exact hour we had agreed to meet at Mr. Branshaw's house, and for that reason, I suggested—rather unsuccessfully, in point of fact—that it would behoove us to have something to eat before we shut ourselves away in a house to listen to the reading of a novel, the length of which was still a mystery to us. But Miss Bunnage was adamant about leaving and wouldn't hear of it. As she took me by the arm she repeated that the carriage was waiting, and I had no other choice but to follow her outside. Once we were off, she finally seemed to calm down a bit; that was when I noticed that she had with her a folder filled with a sheaf of papers.

"Do you think Mr. Branshaw would give me something to eat if I asked him?" I wondered aloud.

Miss Bunnage smiled and replied: "Don't worry, I'll make sure to ask him." After a pause, she added: "I must tell you, this meeting is extremely important to me. If things work out as I hope, I might be able to prevent a great injustice."

"I thought you were simply interested in Victor Arledge."

"Yes, that's right."

"Oh."

I fell silent, amused and annoyed at the same time.

Mr. Branshaw welcomed us into his home with a far more amiable disposition than he had exhibited the previous evening at my party, the consequences of which were beginning to feel intolerable, for the moment at least. After ushering us into a spacious library lined with white bookcases, he busied himself preparing me some breakfast at the almost objectionable insistence of Miss Bunnage, whose behavior, on more than one occasion, actually caused me to blush. It was during this brief interlude, however, that I was able to inspect his collection of books, and I learned that Mr. Branshaw read strictly philosophy and poetry, and very little in the way of novels. Atop the fireplace, in the spot where one would normally find an unseemly hunting scene or the copy of a Constable painting, there was a massive wooden panel that bore the following inscription:

'Tis to yourself I speak; you cannot know
Him whom I call in speaking such a one,
For you beneath the earth lie buried low,
Which he alone as living walks upon:
You may at times have heard him speak to you,
And often wished perchance that you were he;
And I must ever wish that it were true,
For then you could hold fellowship with me:
But now you hear us talk as strangers, met
Above the room wherein you lie abed;
A word perhaps loud spoken you may get,
Or hear our feet when heavily they tread;
But he who speaks, or him who's spoken to,
Must both remain as strangers still to you.

Miss Bunnage, having settled into what looked like the best chair in the room, had opened her folder, removed a few immaculate sheets of white paper, and, pen in hand, waited with obvious impatience as Branshaw reappeared with a tray and I drank my coffee and ate my toast with raspberry jam. Once I was finished, Branshaw whisked the tray away and left the library, only to reappear moments later bearing the coveted manuscript, bound in navy blue cloth. He shook out the book and placed it on the lap of Miss Bunnage, who simply stared at the cover, and then he passed it over to me. *Voyage Along the Horizon,* it said; somehow it felt inappropriate to peek beyond the front cover. Branshaw, however, took it out of my hands just then, sat down, opened it to page 1, and said, "*Voyage Along the Horizon:* Book One. 'Tis to yourself

I speak…'" And he read through the entire verse.

"Who wrote that poem?" I asked, glancing up at the panel above the fireplace.

Branshaw was about to answer, but Miss Bunnage spoke up first: "Jones Very," she replied, and then added: "Please continue, and from this point on, please, I must ask you to remain silent."

Mr. Branshaw read the verse by Very again, with gusto this time, and following a brief pause, he began to read the book aloud.

It was just after the safe return of the voyage captained by William Speirs Bruce, the veteran medical doctor of the Dundee Whaling Expedition, and also right around the time that Jean Charcot was sending out missives from aboard the *Français* that were the talk of Parisian society, that Kerrigan came up with the idea of organizing an expedition to be made up of men and women of letters—precisely those people who, after devouring the information that came in every day from the Palmer Peninsula, would gossip together in the city's cafés about the audacity of those pioneers and confess their own fervent desires to embark, even if only as dishwashers, on one of those Nordic or British steamships, in search of adventures filled with danger and tedious inconvenience, but also with many thrilling and serendipitous experiences, the retelling of which would no doubt dazzle their friends and readers.

Kerrigan, a charming man who possessed the subconscious of an adolescent rather than that of a man his own age, dreamed up a plan that was outrageous and intriguing from the beginning, and the jovial, carefree spirit of this entire endeavor was no doubt what prompted Victor Arledge—as he ate his breakfast on his terrace and racked his brains for a plausible yet sufficiently convoluted excuse that would free him from attending the premiere of the theatrical adaptation of his latest novel without disappointing the audience too much—to suddenly abandon the prudence and serenity with which he made most of his decisions and surrender to Kerrigan's persuasive arguments. The idea was so very novel and Kerrigan's enthusiasm so very innocent and genuine that at first Arledge could only smile and shake his head. But as his loquacious friend began to fill his imagination with images of extraordinary, exotic adventures and sights, and most especially after Kerrigan very deliberately removed from his billfold a slip of paper with a list of the people who had already agreed to participate in this expedition and very ceremoniously flaunted it before his friend's eyes, Arledge could no longer resist, and his already-weakened defenses came crashing down as he rushed to sign the embarkation card on which his name, address, and nationality were already printed, without the slightest of qualms.

A few days later, when the news became public information, the future passengers of the *Tallahassee* found themselves assailed by journalists from every corner of Europe. The preparations for the voyage, as well as its purpose and nature, were the object of such detailed analysis that the newspapers actually told the expeditioners a number of things they had not known (or, perhaps, had not wanted to know) until then, most specifically the intentions of their captain. The headlines on the front pages described it something like this: "MOST AMBITIOUS LITERARY ENTERPRISE KNOWN TO MAN. A large group of illustrious writers and artists from England and France to embark on a voyage to Antarctica, hoping to produce a literary work and a great musical spectacle based on their experiences at the South Pole."

From the day Kerrigan first called on Victor Arledge to the day of their departure, ten weeks went by and it was during this period, which was enlivened by high spirits and a general sense of eager anticipation, that Arledge found himself obliged to alter his normally sedate pace of life, which was a bit unsettling for him. It wasn't the prospect of such a long trip—the purpose of which he was beginning to seriously doubt—that made him edgy but rather the general chaos and confusion that necessarily surrounded the endeavor: the meetings, usually pointless, so insistently organized by the French participants in an obstinate attempt to beat the entire topic into the ground by preparing for any and all surprises that might present themselves en route; then there was the question of the insatiable reporters who were constantly soliciting interviews (which, it should be noted, he always granted); and finally and most important, Arledge had to struggle with the terrible discomfort brought on by his burning, obsessive desire to eliminate one Léonide Meffre from the list of passengers—in fact, that was the real cause of all the distress and drama that had erupted in his tiny apartment on the Rue Buffault. He nonetheless found himself anxiously awaiting the date of their departure, not just because he was anticipating the trip itself—which, thanks to the whims of his fellow passengers, who were financing the lion's share of the venture, would include a brief cruise through the Mediterranean from Marseilles to Smyrna with port calls in Italy and Greece before skirting the North African coast to Gibraltar and then setting off for the open sea—but because he was anticipating the great satisfaction of once again seeing his good friends Esmond and Clara Handl, the two most brilliant comedic playwrights England had bestowed upon the world, and this happy reunion would take place the very day the *Tallahassee* set sail. Delightful and indefatigable conversationalists, Esmond and Clara had written librettos that were renowned all over Europe and even in parts of America, and their presence on board, which Arledge was already anticipating with delight, would surely add a special touch of grace and wit to the voyage. Arledge was sure that once he got onto the boat, he would be able to settle into his stateroom and resume his placid pace of life in no time, and he envisioned himself whiling away the days strolling on deck in his best clothes, whenever the skies and the rhythms of the sea permitted. In the days and weeks leading up to the departure, however, he often found himself on the verge of losing his patience, which he normally had in abundance. The reason, of course, was that during this period he had been forced to contend with an assortment of people he did not particularly care for: first, he had to answer a flurry of letters that had come in from his German, Polish, Spanish, and Italian editors who, upon hearing that he had joined Kerrigan's venture, wanted to secure the translation rights of the novel that, no doubt, he would write upon return; then he had had to take two bothersome trips out of town to bid his family farewell: one by train, to see his parents, and the other by steamship, to see his sister. After fulfilling these obligations he went back home, where he remained inside for five whole days, consumed by the task of organizing and filing his papers, which until then had been scattered randomly on tables and in drawers, folders, and cabinets all throughout the house.

Naturally, Arledge had nothing to do with the preparations or the organization of the voyage itself—there were experts to take care of that sort of thing—but on occasion he did lend an ear to the long-suffering Captain Kerrigan, who would pour out his frustrations to Arledge whenever the obstacles before him began to seem insurmountable. During these sessions Arledge learned that the British government, through a private agency, had contributed a considerable sum of money to Kerrigan's enterprise, and that a number of private companies had donated all sorts of products as well, including textiles, leathers, soaps, shoes, ice-skates, spark plugs, snowshoes, food, matches, and alcoholic beverages, among other things, thereby reducing the passengers' costs considerably. He also learned that Kerrigan had had a very difficult time locating the three dozen Manchurian ponies that seemed, at least at the moment, rather inappropriate to the venture, but during those final days he was so tired of all the preambles and prepara-

tions that he didn't even bother to ask what they were for. Arledge
had also had to endure the wholly unpleasant visit of an ambitious,
petulant tailor who had been hired to make the heavy clothes that
the passengers would need in the colder regions they would be
visiting; and he also suffered the visit of an overly cordial shoe-
maker who, without giving Arledge a moment to object, expertly
outfitted him for several pairs of boots that were almost shapeless
in their simplicity and overwhelming thickness. After this, for no
apparent reason, because despite (or perhaps because of) the aforementioned defects, all the boots were exceedingly comfortable and
warm, he selected only two pairs of bone-colored boots and put
them aside for Arledge. The truth is, a veritable parade of guests
marched through the front door to Arledge's house: a doctor, who
subjected him to an exhaustive physical examination; several government officials, who tried bullying him into paying a variety of
special taxes to no avail despite their very admirable display of
bureaucratic terminology and threatening language; a Franchard
employee determined to convince him to take out an out-
rageously expensive life-insurance policy; and finally, his notary,
who seemed very alarmed by his imminent departure and suggested that it might be extremely convenient to leave behind a
fully executed will and testament before embarking on such a
perilous adventure. A long etcetera of additional characters, as
Arledge liked to call them, followed these aforementioned visitors
in and out of the house, and he listened to all these vile charlatans
and opportunists with careless indifference at first—they were,
after all, protected by the law—but after a time he dispatched them
with neither hesitation nor courtesy.

Not everything was bothersome and tedious, however: during
those two and a half months, Arledge was able to enjoy Kerrigan's
company much more than he normally did, and this was indeed a
pleasure. He really didn't know very much about Kerrigan, but his
conversation, not to mention the little tales he occasionally told,

always in the most abstract form imaginable, unidentifiable in time and space, were for Arledge an endless book of adventure and peril that allowed him to relive the same intense emotions that he had felt while reading his very first books as a child. Often lacking the precise facts that would have allowed him to situate Kerrigan's stories in some specific place in the world, Arledge actually preferred to envision the captain in the most wildly varied situations and uniforms. At one moment, he might imagine Kerrigan in a white captain's hat, sailing through the seas of China, and then at the next moment he could picture him in a gray uniform at Vicksburg, or laughing at the customs agents at Liverpool, or standing alongside the Black Hand anarchists, or wandering about in the middle of the Arabian desert, or else sauntering through the docks of some port town somewhere, a Cicero in Florence surrounded by beautiful women, the only survivor of the *U.S.S. Maine,* or at Charles George Gordon's side in the Sudan.

In point of fact, there were only four things that Arledge knew for sure about Kerrigan: he was an American; as a young man he had been the captain of a steamboat that sailed up and down the Mississippi River; at some time in his life he had been one-half of a most passionate love story, though Arledge knew nothing of the (surely) tragic details; and he had discovered an island in the Pacific. The exact location of this island was known to nobody but Kerrigan, and it seemed to have a mysterious hold on him, calling him away for countless trips and long, unexplained absences. That was all Arledge, through his discreet, courteous prying techniques, was able to find out: Kerrigan's family, his past, his professional life, and most important, the origin of his tremendous fortune, which allowed him to live quite comfortably without having to do a thing, remained a mystery. His spoken English was somewhat deformed from all his travels, but it nevertheless retained an accent that revealed the very lofty social class to which he belonged, and his conversation, always agile and clever, suggested that he possessed the kind of knowledge that would have been difficult to acquire amid oceans, deserts, battles, and international conspiracies. Although white and gold blended indiscriminately atop his head and in his moustache, he was most definitely no older than fifty, and his slender, muscular physique made him seem far younger than his years. His excessively flamboyant clothing choices were a clear indication of his poor taste, and the tall boots he insisted on wearing made an exceeding amount of noise as he walked, but in terms of mannerisms and customs, he was a perfect, flawless gentleman. His popularity in Paris, where he had been living since 1899, was tremendous, and his presence was all but required at just about every important social occasion, for he was the delight of countless insufferable society dowagers who, like Mme D'Almeida, fed his vanity and, on occasion, even endangered his life with their frequently indiscreet and inopportune gossip.

Kerrigan, however, did not get along very well with the majority of the illustrious French explorers. He may have enjoyed their sympathies, but the feeling was not mutual, and he tended to treat them with a restrained tolerance that occasionally bordered on very barely concealed disdain that manifested itself through a sudden curtness that his companions often dismissed as mere eccentricity, but that Arledge felt was his way of expressing his devastating feelings of disillusion and sadness. At those moments, there was nothing anyone could do to bring back the broad smile on his face. He would just look around for the nearest chair and settle down in it for a long while, almost in a meditative state, and his face would curl into a scowl that indicated a deep sense of dissatisfaction with everything around him. These long silences, which were usually followed by sudden trips to lands bathed by the sea, were not common, but they had grown slightly more frequent during the months leading up to his morning visit at Rue Buffault. This mood may have been inspired by the recent publication, in a British magazine, of an article about Americans living in Europe. Written under a pseudonym, the article included several unkind comments about Kerrigan ("an overgrown adventurer who tries to attract attention to himself by exploiting certain mysteries about his life, when in reality, after five comfortable, peaceful years in Paris, he is perhaps best-known for being the reigning prince of the city's nightlife, completely bereft of ambition and quite averse to taking any kind of risks...") and for this reason, in addition to his genuine enthusiasm for Kerrigan's plan, Arledge was also cheered because he once again saw his friend filled with gusto, overflowing with energy, his eyes sparkling. Kerrigan truly despised the other passengers, and this was no doubt the reason that he suddenly began confiding all his problems to the English author living in France as time ticked away and the *Tallahassee*'s departure loomed on the horizon. And though there was nothing Arledge could do to help him resolve these problems, he did give Kerrigan a chance to return to the past and to the landscapes against which his childhood had unfolded, and this in the end was what helped bring Kerrigan's momentary flights of anger to a relatively rapid conclusion. The slightly reserved friendship between the two men grew less distant and more intense during this time, though it never reached the bothersome and uncomfortable extremes that truly close friendships inevitably produce.

This collection of inconveniences and surprises—all of which were brought about by the same motivating factor: their desire to leave—was soon complicated by yet another odd turn of events that, having been prompted by something truly undesirable, eventually came to rob Arledge of his sleep for more than a few nights. The "something," if you will, was curiosity, and in the case of Victor Arledge curiosity had become a veritable method and way of life for as long as he could remember. His curiosity, in this case, was piqued by one of his future travel companions, a British gentleman who had captured his attention for a most unusual reason. Hugh Everett Bayham, the son of a wealthy landowner and a fixture on London's nightlife, was a promising young pianist who lived in the English capital, and was married to the well-known actress Margaret Holloway. It was not, however, any of these vulgar, typical, and meaningless facts that caused Arledge's ears to prick up every time the pianist's name was mentioned in his presence. No, not at all. As it happened, shortly before Kerrigan dreamed up the idea for the Antarctic voyage, Esmond Handl had written Arledge a long letter—they usually wrote to one another about once every two months—recounting the story of a very odd circumstance involving Bayham, the young pianist. As soon as Arledge finished reading the tale he was overcome by the urge to move to London and, via Handl, somehow manage to procure a meeting with Bayham, such was the fascination that the story had sparked in his mind. But Arledge's innate curiosity was matched and perhaps even overcompensated by a propensity for sloth that dissuaded him from doing anything about it, and the topic soon fell from his mind, though not for long. A week after he had signed the embarkation card that confirmed his participation in the *Tallahassee* adventure, Kerrigan informed him that four English musicians had agreed to join the expedition. And one of those musicians was Hugh Everett Bayham. From that moment on, spurred by the possibility of meeting him face-to-face, Arledge's interest was not only revived but was growing more fervent with each passing day. Once he had managed to dig Handl's letter out from under the towering piles of correspondence in his office, he placed the missive in a prominent spot on his work desk, and read it over and over again in the days to come.

My dear friend,
For once I am pleased to forgo the typical and horribly tedious bits of news regarding our activities with which I normally bore you. On this occasion, I have something far more interesting to write you about; in fact, I am certain that you will find the story I am

about to tell you most satisfying and intriguing. I am so convinced
of this, dear friend, that I am permitting myself to savor your appreciation even before you yourself can express it. Nevertheless, before
I go any further, and to ensure that at least one small part of this letter seems something other than utterly mad to you, let me quickly
say that Clara is in perfect health after a very mild respiratory ail-
ment that kept her in bed for ten days, that everything is moving
brilliantly ahead with us as well, that *Goodbye, Dear Barbara* has gone
from strength to strength with the public and the critics, that
Margaret Holloway has finally deigned to try her hand at comedy
and has agreed to star in our next piece along with Roger Gaylord,
and that I wish you all the glory and recognition you deserve at the
Theatre Antoine. I say all this, in part, to prove that it is I and not
an impostor who writes this letter, for you might guess as much
once you read the truly startling story of Hugh Everett Bayham, a
good if rather recently cultivated friend, a musician of peerless talent, a man of great—though not excessive—imagination, and a
continental figure who, as you may recall, I mentioned in my last
letter to you, when I described our first meeting.

Very well, then. Bayham is a man who likes to indulge in long
evening walks, alone, through the streets of our beloved city, and this
indulgence becomes a regular habit when his evening activities
include one of his rather theatrical, somewhat unwieldy, and no
doubt exhausting performances. About two weeks ago, after a truly
extraordinary concert (Brahms and Clementi) and the gushing
accolades that followed, Bayham, as he always did, said good night to
one and all at the door to the concert hall, got into a carriage with
his wife, and, after seeing her safely home, set out on his evening
walk. Little did he—or we, for that matter—know that for the next
four days we would all be racking our brains—which, under normal
circumstances, we surely could have dedicated to other, less troubling
and more leisurely pursuits—trying to figure out where he was. As
it turned out, Margaret Holloway awoke the following day to find

herself completely alone in bed, and from that moment on none of us had a moment of peace. Margaret all but forced us to comb every last street, public house, and private residence in London—though to this end I will allow myself to skip over my own inquiries, for they were filled with the kind of infelicitous surprises and embarrassing situations that a person like myself should never have to experience—and then she notified the police, who, despite their superior experience and expert tools for carrying out this type of investigation, had no better luck than we had.

It was toward the end of the fourth day, by which time Margaret was firmly in the clutches of a dreadful attack of hysteria, that Bayham appeared at my house. Margaret was with us, sobbing away uncontrollably, when he turned up, clean, freshly bathed, and impeccably dressed. As I opened the door, he smiled at me, shook my hand, and then, slightly puzzled, asked why I was so tired, for the fatigue of the previous four days very clearly showed on my face. Then he walked into the sitting room, greeted his wife with an affectionate though rather perfunctory embrace, and after insisting that we all sit down, removed a cigarette from his jacket pocket, lit it, and began to speak. This is what he had to say:

"I suppose, my dear friends, given your very obvious astonishment here this morning, you will now be expecting a detailed explanation of what has happened to me over the past few days. And given that I am a well-known figure, if not quite a household name of course, I am glad to see that my very first explanation of the events, which I owe first and foremost to my wife, will also be heard by others. This way, perhaps, I may be able to avoid having to retell the story over and over again, for I have no doubt that it will be of great interest to our friends, all of whom have been so terribly worried by my absence and, for the same reason, I fear, will demand the relative satisfaction of an explanation. For this reason, and not wishing to cause any of you the slightest bother, I will be eternally grateful if you would excuse Margaret and me—for we are both still quite agitated and nervous as the result of what we have recently endured—from that obligation which, despite its indubitable charms, may well turn out to be terribly boring in the end."

"For goodness' sake, Hugh, enough quibbling!" exclaimed Margaret.

Hugh shot her a withering look and replied: "My dear, I need not remind you just where your testy temperament has gotten us in the past. So please, allow me to continue as I see fit." And picking up right where he left off, as if the interruption had never occurred at all, he went on: "Now, bear in mind that it will not be easy for me to give you a clear and complete account of everything that has happened over these past four days, given that I myself am not entirely certain of it all. Nevertheless, with certain reservations— not involving the story itself but rather the vocabulary used by one of the people involved and certain episodes which I must necessarily abbreviate in consideration of the ladies present—I will attempt to give you a picture of what transpired.

"The entire story began before I had scarcely walked five hundred paces from the door to my house, before the night air could even begin to chase the odor of tobacco from my suit. A carriage, drawn by two horses, promptly began to follow me down the road, though I didn't realize this until I stopped for a moment to look into a store window, at which point I heard it come to a stop alongside me. A door opened, and I heard a voice call out, 'Mr. Hugh Everett Bayham, sir?'

"Now, it is not uncommon for music aficionados to occasionally recognize me on the street and call out a greeting, so I turned around, not at all surprised, expecting to find myself facing one of them, or else an acquaintance of some sort, but because of the poor illumination on the road, combined with the very dark upholstery of the coach, I was able to discern only what seemed to be a very elegant gentleman's suit and the hint of a face with very fine, evenly proportioned features.

"'That's correct, sir. With whom do I have the pleasure of speaking?' I replied.

"'Mr. Bayham,' the gentleman answered. 'As you may have noticed, I have been following you for some time without daring to approach you, so, so...'

"'Oh no, no,' I interrupted him. 'I didn't notice a thing. How may I be of assistance to you?'

"'Sir, Mr. Bayham, this is neither the time nor the place for such introductions. The matter that has forced me to approach you in such an unorthodox manner is too urgent and too grave. I beg of you, however, to step at once into my carriage, where we may be more comfortable and better disposed to have a brief conversation. Please.'

"In the space of fifteen seconds an exhaustive process of evaluation took place inside my mind: if I got into the carriage, I would run the risk of regretting it later on; if I did not get in, such a risk did not exist, which meant I would most definitely regret not doing so later on. So I got in. The gentleman offered me his hand for support, and despite the glove that covered it, I felt as though I were touching something very soft and cold that crumbled between my fingers as gelatin would. The contact between our hands was brief and inconsequential, and I did not pay it the slightest attention. I then sat down next to the gentleman, whose face I could now see with clarity (graying hair, wide temples, gray eyes, arched brows, straight nose), and I asked him, 'Well?'

"I was not, however, granted a reply. At that moment, the gentleman gave a rapid order to his driver, who duly transmitted the order to his two horses with his whip, and the two beasts broke into a gallop. That was when I realized that these were not two normal draught animals nor were they the typical Percheron horses that one is accustomed to seeing in the city. They were racehorses, without a doubt, and they were now, quite literally, racing down the deserted city streets, and the violent swaying of the carriage slammed me over and over against the body of the gentleman, who was also swinging wildly against the walls of the vehicle, to such a degree that I was unable to even utter a complaint or protest, for I was so occupied with the simple task of not losing my balance. The journey continued on like this for some ten minutes until, finally, the horses slowed down, and I saw that we were approaching Victoria Station. Right then, the carriage came to a stop, and before I had a chance to gather myself after such a diabolical ride or voice my indignation at such treatment, two men pulled me outside and very nearly dragged me to a platform where a train was already departing. Running alongside the moving train, they pushed me inside, and I saw that the gentleman, who had been following closely behind us, also boarded the train though with a certain amount of difficulty. They then dragged me, with the same merciless treatment as before, to an empty compartment which they shut with a deadbolt, and they brusquely threw me onto one of the seats. The gentleman (though perhaps I ought not think of him as such) sat down directly in front of me, and the two other men sat down next to me, one on either side. Right away, one of them began to shower insults upon my person in a thick Scottish brogue that rendered most of his words incomprehensible to me, though I did hear him accuse me of being an opportunist. His language was intolerable and his voice, which would plague me for several nights thereafter in the form of a recurring nightmare, was insufferably piercing and coarse. After four or five minutes, however, he calmed down and finally stopped talking. For once, there was total silence in the compartment and I, for one, was not inclined to try to fill it in any way. They had not threatened me with weapons, nor had they coerced me with words, but given the very effective savagery with which they executed the kidnapping—I believe I can call it as such, despite everything—and their categorical certainty as to the legitimacy of the things they did and said to me, not to mention their clearly violent attitudes, I was frightened beyond belief. Only after ten more minutes had passed, and it had become clear that none of the three men was interested in giving me any kind of explanation, or even instructions, I was emboldened to utter something, if rather timidly: 'What is the meaning of this, gentlemen? There must be some mistake...'

"'Silence!' cried the gentleman, and as he said this, the man who had previously been insulting me began to strike me with a blunt object that I couldn't quite see.

"'But please, at least tell me why...' I sputtered, in another attempt to discover what was happening.

"This time it was the gentleman who lashed out at me, slapping me across the face. As you can imagine, since all of you know perfectly well that I am of a rather sluggish character, and an admirer of subtlety, the prospect of any kind of violence or physical harm strikes terror in my heart. Because of this, my very theoretical and by now quite debilitated valor evaporated into thin air after this last turn of events. And so, at that moment, I decided not to utter another word unless I was spoken to first, and to simply watch and wait as the events unfolded. This private decision brought some measure of relief to my suffering body and some measure of rest, if not clarity, to my troubled mind. Perhaps you will find it strange that I could be overcome by sleep at such a trying moment, but I was. Do bear in mind that scarcely two hours earlier I had been playing Brahms in concert, and that fatigue can be far more powerful than fear and tension at times. It didn't even occur to me, oddly enough, that salvation might come my way in the form of a conductor or ticket agent who, one could only assume, would have to appear sooner or later. Nor did I think much about kidnapping, and the various ways it can be carried out. My assailants had lowered the window curtain, depriving me even of the minor consolation and distraction of gazing out at the nighttime landscape. By the time my eyes were closed, I had fully accepted the facts: I neither understood them nor approved of them, but I accepted them and would even venture to say that, at that moment, I still did not regret having entered the carriage. I still don't—or at least, I don't believe I do. In any event, all of this was an amorphous collection of vague, ephemeral ideas that paraded endlessly through my mind, and I did nothing in particular to stop them from taking their course.

"By the time I awoke it was morning, and the air was heavy with the pungent aroma of heather. When I looked out the window—the curtain was raised now—I was greeted by a rural landscape that I guessed might be Scottish, dappled as it was in hues of green and gray. Having recovered a certain level of good humor—to the extent that this was at all possible—I turned to my companions and said: 'Good morning, gentlemen.'

"None of the men, all of whom were now (perhaps still) awake, responded, and so I decided to concentrate my energies on studying each of them as closely as possible: the gentleman, whose face I had been able to make out before I had fallen prey to their ruse the previous evening, seemed like an educated man, and his gaze, though cold and slightly sickening, seemed to suggest intelligence. The other two men, who wore peaked caps and white trench coats, were so vulgar and boorish that I doubt I would remember them if I were ever to cross paths with them again.

"More than an hour had gone by since the train had last stopped at a station, and I began to fear that the trip was never going to end. The string of train cars was snaking its way around a coastline that was entirely unfamiliar to me when, all of a sudden, it came to a halt at a station in a village so modest and unremarkable that the train station did not even bear a sign indicating its name. The stop lasted no more than a few minutes, and once the train started off again, the three men jumped up and grabbed me by the arms, and in no time at all we all leaped off the train together. As the train lumbered off into the distance we ran through that ramshackle depot as quickly as we had raced through Victoria Station, and got into a rickety carriage that was waiting for us outside. The gentleman, the brute who had insulted me, and I sat inside, while the other brute sat outside, in front, next to the driver. Next, they placed a black blindfold around my eyes, despite my reiterated protests—after all, if there was anything to be gained from such a bizarre experience, it was the landscape, which was truly quite breathtaking—and I sensed that we then passed through a very small village before turning onto a narrow, rocky path. Later on, I felt the carriage wheels begin to dig their way through what felt like sand, and as the carriage approached the sea, the sand gave way to mud, which further complicated the carriage's movements. That was where my journey came to an end. From there, I was ordered to step down from the carriage, and then the two brutes shoved me from behind until I finally entered a house, tripping up two steps and across a porch. Inside, I breathed in a lovely floral scent that wafted through the air, and my feet sank into a rug of some sort. Those are the last two clear and totally accurate recollections I have. Then, suddenly, someone struck me on the back of my neck, and I suppose I lost consciousness at that point. And this, dear Margaret, dear friends, marks the beginning of the period about which I know nothing. I cannot offer you any kind of detail regarding the things I am about to describe, because when I woke up, I found that I had lost all sense of time, and I did not regain it until just now, when I bought a newspaper and discovered that four days had gone by since the evening I accepted the invitation from the gentleman in the carriage. These past three days have been far too confusing for me to be able to give you a coherent and chronologically accurate explanation of what happened. I can only describe the feelings I felt, the experiences I had, and the woman who seduced me.

"They brought me to a sitting room filled with books and old country furniture—selected with exceedingly good taste, I might add—on the second floor of a rambling home, the façade of which I never managed to see, though I could tell it was very close to the sea. And though I spent many long hours in that room, I cannot describe it to you with any precision, nor can I name a single one of the books piled up on the bookshelves, even though I do recall that, on occasion, I spent time reading some of them. I believe I slept quite often, which would explain, at least partially, why I thought I had been locked up for months inside that spacious, airy room. Every so often, the man who had insulted me on the train would come by with a tray bearing either milk or beer, bread or meat, soup or vegetables, which he would deposit on a table before taking advantage of his time with me to beat me around the shoulders and shower me with more of his unmentionable language in a brogue that, unfortunately, was not quite so incomprehensible any more. On more than one occasion I could hear the sound of female voices—that happy, idle hum of women amusing themselves. You see, in addition to the gentleman, the house was most definitely occupied by three or four women, and all of them, with the possible exception of one, were very young. Though I was never able to discern the exact words they said to one another as they floated up from a lower floor, I could tell from their tone of voice, from the very pleasurable murmurs that reached my ears, and from the cadence of their conversations, that the group was composed of a mother and her daughters—two or three, I can't be sure. One of them played the piano constantly, and her repertoire and skills were impressive and masterful. The sound of the music reached my room through the floorboards and the windows, and though I stuck my head out the window several times in the hope of catching even the tiniest glimpse of the room directly beneath my own—risking not only a terrible fall but the possibility of being caught by one of the men from the train, who kept a constant watch over my windows from their post outside the mansion—I was never able to discern much more than the far right-hand side of the keyboard of a piano that rested against a wall and, every once in a while, the right hand of the young lady who played it, her fingers traveling gently across the keys. I also spent many long hours with my ears pressed against the wall, trying to decipher the things they said, though with little success. The only time I recognized anything they said was when the young lady began playing a new piece; at that moment I would suddenly realize that one of the many words I had just heard was, in fact, the name of the composer. The atmosphere that seemed to envelop those brief musical recitals, though only vaguely perceptible, seemed to be that of a family piano lesson. What I mean is that the young lady was clearly a very promising music student—perhaps too promising—and the rest of her family—the mother, the sisters, and only rarely the father, whose voice I identified as that of the gentleman from the carriage—were always all too delighted to attend the young woman's brilliant practice sessions, which they clearly found utterly captivating. To occupy myself during these long hours, I would place my hands on a table and move my fingers in time to whatever piece the young lady played, and on more than one occasion I found myself overcome by the most desperate urge to abandon my table, leave the room, rush downstairs, and take over the young lady's piano—or better yet, play the pieces she selected with her at my side, our four hands traveling across the keyboard together. Right now I cannot remember the exact pieces she played, but I can say that the majority of them were very well known. I do remember one occasion, however, that was completely different from all the rest. One of the guards suddenly came up to my room and closed the shutters so that I would no longer be able to open them from the inside. Weak as I was, stretched out on the bed, I simply let him do as he wished, idly wondering what had prompted this change. Shortly thereafter, a flurry of muffled voices began to reach my ears—far more than normal, as if a group of people had gathered downstairs in anticipation of something. Then, quite abruptly, everything went silent, and after a few moments I heard the first notes of Schumann's Violin and Piano Sonata in D minor. A recital, it seemed, was underway. I believe this took place on the second day of my captivity but, I must insist, I cannot be certain. The violin, I hypothesized, was being played either by one of the guests—the arrival of whom I had been prohibited from seeing, which was obvious enough at this point—or by the gentleman from the carriage who possibly only played the instrument on special occasions. In any event, the piece eventually came to an end and was followed by a brief pause, during which time I could hear the clinking glasses and coughs one always hears during concert intermissions. A few seconds later, the young woman's piano and her father's violin began to play the Kreutzer Sonata. I could scarcely believe my ears, for it was altogether clear that these two amateur musicians could have easily played alongside the most accomplished professionals, and I could not help but admire them tremendously. That was when I began to wonder if perhaps my kidnapping had been prompted by the envy of one of my rivals, or perhaps the excessive enthusiasm of some music aficionado who, later on— given that I am here with you now—regretted having put me through such a despicable experience. I am afraid that I will never know the answer to that mystery. All these memories are so vague and so incredible that I suspect my captors slipped some kind of narcotic into the milk they made me drink, or else—who knows?—perhaps they injected me with some substance as I slept. Despite all this, the time I spent in that house was terribly monotonous, for my sole visitor was that brute who came in only to hit me—that is, until my last day there, which seems to have been yesterday, given that it is one of the few things I am able to remember with any clarity, aside from the violin and piano sonatas. I believe I was in the middle of reading a tediously dull novel by Thackeray, listening to a lovely piano piece that the young woman had most certainly composed herself, when the door opened and a girl, about fifteen years old, entered the room and walked over to me. Her blue eyes exuded sweetness and wit, and her long black hair, which tumbled down over her bare shoulders, framed a pale face with delicate

features and prominent cheekbones. I cannot recall if she said anything, nor do I remember what happened after her lips brushed
mine for the first time—and that, I must admit, is something I most
certainly recall quite effortlessly. Please forgive me, ladies, for the
rather unseemly nature of my account. I would never dream of
offending you, and I trust that I haven't done so, because I do
believe it is perfectly clear that the state I was in had absolutely no
relation to me or my true sentiments, and I know—though perhaps
I ought not presume—that you would never question the story I
am telling you and think it a figment of my imagination. I must
confess, however, that whether it was a dream or a real mansion on
the Scottish coast, I made no protest. The young woman then left
the room, and I fell into a deep, long sleep, my slumber serenaded
by the lovely notes her sister played on the piano.

"This morning when I woke up I was at Maidstone, lying on
the grass in a park, with enough money in my pocket to pay for my
return trip to London. Perhaps you believe what I say, perhaps not;
I am fully aware that my story sounds terribly implausible and unworthy of your attention, but on my word of honor I swear that is
how I remember it. Here is my ticket from Maidstone; my clothes
are at my house, unwashed, in tatters, covered with holes and filled
with sand; my shoulders are black and blue, and there is even a slight
swelling on the back of my neck. Tomorrow I plan to get a full medical examination to determine whether I was, in fact, drugged, and
I have already alerted the police so that they may begin to carry out
the appropriate investigations. As far as everything else is concerned,
I feel perfectly fine, and I can only presume that all of this has been
a terrible mistake on the part of my kidnappers, who, upon realizing
their error, freed me at once. It is all over now, and I do hope this
matter is never again discussed in my presence. Let us take it in
stride, and for my part I will make every attempt to relegate the
events of these past four days, indelible but innocuous, to my memory. Thank you for hearing me out, dear Esmond and Clara."

The following day, a doctor examined Hugh Everett Bayham with an eye to all that he suspected might have been done to him, and the police continued investigating the case, though without any conclusive results. Of course, everyone in town is quite taken by the story, which they, by and large, believe to be true—except, naturally, the episode with the young lady. I, of course, feel particularly honored to have heard the direct version of the story, in exclusive, as it were. I have only seen Hugh and Margaret once since the day he returned, just as we were leaving the theater one evening, and while they may have seemed a tad more serious and perhaps less chatty than usual, it did look as though they had put the incident behind them.

And that, my dear Victor, is all I can think of to tell you about today. I anxiously await news from you and, of course, if there is any new light you might be able to shed on this matter, I will communicate it to you at once.

Fond regards from Clara and best wishes from your friend, Esmond Handl.

No new light, as it turned out, was to be shed on the matter. Arledge, like Handl and his friends, was convinced that at least part of the story had to be a lie, but he was not inclined, as they were, to doubt the existence of the young woman. Arledge was certain that Handl had rendered Bayham's words verbatim, for Esmond had a special talent for reciting, from memory, word for word, the lines of any character from any play he had ever seen—even once. What most captured Arledge's attention was the way the pianist spoke—his impertinent ease at the beginning of his tale; his dramatic pause in the middle as he tried to underscore the ambiguous nature of the events that followed; his sudden gravity as he described the young woman and the way she had suddenly appeared in his room; his earnest efforts to come up with proof that his facts were accurate; and then the indifferent, remorseless attitude he displayed toward his wife after four days of agonizing separation... all

these things made Arledge wonder if the half-week Hugh Everett
Bayham had spent outside of London had affected him more than
he realized, and this hypothesis only made him want to meet Bayham even more. These impulses, along with some other ones, perhaps more hidden and sinister, quickly turned the voyage into an
obsession for Arledge.

Fearful that the answer might dissuade him from participating
altogether, Arledge preferred not to know exactly how long the
journey was supposed to last, but the moment did arrive, about ten
days before they were due to set sail, when he realized that the fan-
ciful images with which Kerrigan had tempted and persuaded him
to join the expedition that morning in his apartment on the Rue
Buffault had begun to seem far less intriguing than before, and at
times they even escaped his mind altogether. Never did he actually
stop and think of the *Tallahassee* as a place that would become his
"home" for any extended period of time, nor did he ever acknowledge the expedition for what it really was (the brief
Mediterranean cruise aside, of course): a pompous attempt to
penetrate the depths of Antarctica beyond the limits reached by
Bruce, Larsen, Scott, and Nordenskjöld. And while the rest of the
voyagers spent most of their time leading up to the trip gathering
information about previous expeditions to the South Pole and
learning techniques for saving their fellow passengers in the event
the ground cracked beneath their feet and they were tossed to the
mercy of the glacial waters, Arledge did not bother himself with
such preparations, aside from his efforts—which began the day he
learned he would have the pleasure of meeting Hugh Everett
Bayham in Marseilles—to eliminate someone by the name of
Léonide Meffre from the list of passengers. And so, ten days earlier,
when Kerrigan came to call at his house, in terribly dour spirits
after one of his most popular English passengers had voided his
embarkation card, Arledge very nonchalantly asked the name of
the traveler, and as he valiantly tried to keep his emotions under

control, he realized that the one and only reason he was participating in the expedition was his now frantic need to learn what
had really happened to Hugh Everett Bayham in Scotland. Kerrigan's reply was soothing to Arledge's ears in more way than one,
for it offered a morsel of information that served to confirm the
very sinister nature of the English pianist's kidnapping: Margaret
Holloway, it turned out, had separated from her husband and thus
would not be participating in the expedition after all.

The day that witnessed the departure of the *Tallahassee*—a sailboat
with a metal hull, three masts, and a steam engine, classified by
Lloyds Register of Shipping as a mixed vessel, property of the
Cunard White Star, built by Newport News Shipbuilding and Dry
Dock Company in the United States, purchased by Great Britain
(where it was newly registered in 1896, though its original name,
that of the city where it was baptized, remained the same), capable
of reaching a velocity of 11.5 knots, with capacity for seventy passengers, and operating under the command of Ship's Captain
Eustace Seebohm, Englishman, and First Officer J. D. Kerrigan,
American—there was a great celebration at the port of Marseilles.
The ship was fêted and festooned with balloons, confetti, and
streamers that dappled the surrounding waters with their dazzling
colors. As they boarded the vessel one by one, the passengers were
cheered by the onlookers. Finally, at ten in the morning, after all the
obligatory ceremonies had finally come to a close, the boat pushed
away from the coast with forty-two prominent society figures, fifteen men of science, and an inevitably furious, resentful crew.

BOOK THREE

Victor Arledge had grown so bored that he had lost almost all interest in the journey when, all of a sudden, the boatswain disappeared. Until then, monotony and the rather foolish female passengers had taken over everything on board, dashing the men's plans to take wild risks and embark on uncharted adventures. To make matters worse, the women also dominated all the activity on the upper deck. From the second day of the voyage onward, Esmond Handl had had to hole up in his stateroom, having fallen prey to the rocking of the boat, and his wife Clara (with a selflessness that bordered on that very insufferable kind solemnity with which people often treat the elderly) had vanished along with him. Kerrigan was far too absorbed in his own activities, his rapport with the ladies on board, and his concerns as to the health of his Manchurian ponies. Bayham, to Arledge's great chagrin, spent his days and most of his nights playing whist in the smoking lounge, and when he did not—an unusual occasion indeed—he could generally be found strolling on deck or gazing out at the water with a misty look in his eyes, in the company of a very lovely young woman with black hair who, it should be noted, very rarely allowed herself to be seen on deck alone and whose identity was a mystery to Arledge. This effectively dissuaded Arledge from trying to cultivate a friendship or even a conversation with Bayham; for that, he would have either had to learn the very boring rudiments of card games or make idle chitchat with two people to whom he had never been introduced, thanks to Handl's illness as well as the notion—held by all the passengers except for the one who actually thought about such things—that all the people on the boat were already somehow intimately acquainted with one another. Not even Léonide Meffre deigned to irritate him with his vulgar observations. He had been completely overcome by lethargy, and the only attention he received was from a group of overbearing matrons who fawned over him and plied him with all sorts of warnings and practical advice, more than anything to have something to say to someone other than themselves. The researchers, on the other hand, put him to sleep with their dense, meticulous descriptions of Antarctica, filled with the kind of scholarship and technical details that did not interest him in the least. The one person whose presence was in fact less constant than he might have wished, and whose calm, extremely serene presence convinced him not to heed his recurring urge to abandon the ship at the next port of call, was an older British gentleman who had earned something of a reputation for the short stories he wrote under the *nom de plume* of Tourneur. A man of delicate health and a simple, broad face, he could always be found in the company of his aging wife, sitting on one of the wicker or canvas lounge chairs that dotted the upper deck. The ports of call, incidentally, had given rise to some very heated debate as well as a general, inevitable amount of grumbling afterward. Kerrigan, Seebohm, and the men of science felt that the fewer and the faster the stops the better, for their priority was to move ahead with the journey as quickly as possible. A considerable number of passengers, however, who would be disembarking at Tangiers before returning to their respective homes, demanded continuous stops all along the way. As a result of these divergent opinions—Captain Seebohm's perspective on things held little sway over the passengers, who were after all paying his salary—it was decided that the *Tallahassee* would stop at all the coastal cities of Italy, Greece, and Turkey for a few hours or, in some very exceptional cases, a day. The general atmosphere of discontent, however, exacerbated by the matrons' thinly veiled bickering and the crew's never-ending protests, often began to boil over. On these occasions, the Tourneurs and Arledge tried suggesting that the captain change course entirely and head for the Suez Canal, Ethiopia, and India, but they never mustered much support and, their energy flagging as the days wore on, they had no other choice but to endure the insipid cruise to which they had condemned themselves. Tourneur and his wife, Marjorie, were among those passengers who would be staying behind in Tangiers—not for lack of adventure, but because of the writer's weak constitution, which required them to live in only the hottest of climates— and just as Arledge contemplated this potentially disastrous panorama and began to consider seriously the idea of abandoning ship with them, even though doing so would mean abandoning the Scottish enigma and all that went along with it, a boatswain suddenly disappeared, and from that moment on, the expedition took an unexpected twist as the passengers of the *Tallahassee* were now genuinely interested, if not intrigued, to see what might happen next on this strange voyage they had all embarked on together. Arledge himself had never personally met the boatswain, who was known to be an extremely foul-tempered man, but then again he had never had any contact with any other crew members, either, for that matter. During his many hours of leisure on the upper deck, however, he had observed the boatswain insulting and mistreating his subordinates on several occasions, and based on this he could only guess that someone had dragged the man from his bunk one night, tied a rock around his neck, and tossed him into the water. There was, of course, no evidence to prove that such a thing had actually occurred—and had Arledge come across any, he certainly wouldn't have shared it with the authorities—and so Seebohm, who was responsible for the boatswain as well as everyone else on board, attempted to assuage the fears of his passengers by declaring that the boatswain had most likely deserted the expedition. This was a highly dubious hypothesis, given the fact that Collins—that was the name of the boatswain—truly seemed to take pleasure in his job, his abuses, and the excesses produced by his mood swings.

Things remained more or less at a standstill until they reached Alexandria, which was a territory under British jurisdiction in those days. As soon as she entered the port, the *Tallahassee* was subjected to an inspection by the police, led by a decrepit old infantry colonel and veteran of the Battle of Inkerman who did not look as if he were planning to retire anytime soon. Climbing onto the sailboat with a firm gait and a stern, grumpy expression on his face, the police chief asked to speak with the ship's captain. Seebohm and Kerrigan came out to greet him and, after they were officially introduced to Colonel McLiam, chief of the British Police in Alexandria, the three men went into Captain Seebohm's office.

"Very well, Captain Seebohm," McLiam began. "I understand you've lost one of your crew."

"That's correct, Colonel," replied Seebohm, slightly hesitant.

"And yet you have not reported the incident," Colonel McLiam continued.

"That is correct, sir," Kerrigan volunteered. "We planned to do it here."

"But you sailed past Cyprus, which is under British jurisdiction," replied McLiam. "You should have alerted the authorities there."

"It was not one of our scheduled ports of call, sir, and we have already called at far too many ports on this trip as it is, causing us to lose a great deal of time, and we thought it convenient to wait until we reached Alexandria," replied Kerrigan. "Has Collins turned up anywhere?"

"Is that his name? Collins? What was his position?"

"He was the boatswain, sir."

"An officer? Gentleman, this is far more serious than I thought. His body was just found near the port. Captain Seebohm, your officer was murdered. But what I fail to understand is how his body could have suddenly appeared at Alexandria when he disappeared before you even reached Nicosia."

"I have no idea, sir, but we are missing one of our boats," Seebohm lied, no doubt fully aware of the dire consequences his negligence had caused. "It's possible that it may have been attacked by Turkish bandits. Their field of influence extends quite far, I understand—I know for a fact that they've been spotted close to Port Said on more than one occasion, for example. In any case, what was the cause of death?"

"There was a bullet wound to the head, but we also found several lacerations on his neck, possibly abrasions from a very rough rope. That, in fact, seems to be the real cause of death. His neck was practically torn to shreds."

"Well, then, it's quite possible that the Turks hanged him and then finished off the work by shooting him in the head."

"Just a moment. First of all, the bullet wound was in the neck, and I never said he was hanged or strangled, just that he had some very deep gashes on his neck that were not produced by a knife. As for everything else, yes, I do suppose it was probably the work of some Turkish rogues who tortured him until he expired. In any case, I'm sorry to inform you that you won't be able to set sail again until further notice from me. I'll be waiting for you at my headquarters in two hours, gentlemen: twelve o'clock on the dot. I'll need some personal information from both of you, and I also have to ask you to identify the body and submit an official report regarding the boatswain's disappearance. I trust you've already drafted something. Collins had no identification on his person, and when we found him the only clothes he had on were his trousers. In his pockets all we found was some loose tobacco and three packs of cigarettes, the kind distributed for free, to publicize a trip or event of some sort. The word *Tallahassee* was printed on the cigarette boxes—that's how we realized you'd lost a man." He paused. "Well, then. Until noon, gentlemen."

As soon as McLiam disembarked, panic rapidly spread among the scientists as Kerrigan relayed the details of the conversation. Seriously alarmed now, they peppered him with questions, all but demanding his assurance that no bandits—from Turkey or any other neighboring country—were anywhere near the vessel, that the colonel's visit had been a figment of his imagination, and that they would be able to move ahead with their expedition as planned. The other passengers, who had missed McLiam's arrival on board but were drawn by the ensuing commotion, were now milling about on the upper deck, clamoring for an explanation. Some of the women ventured to suggest that the most prudent thing to do would be to end the journey right then and there, and wait in Alexandria until they could return to Europe in the company of British military escorts. As all this was happening on the upper deck, Seebohm called a meeting of his officers, whose code of responsibility and duty was questionable at best, and he gave them strict orders to acknowledge, in the event they were ever questioned, that one of the *Tallahassee*'s boats had indeed gone missing.

Arledge decided to get away from the agitated crowd and headed toward the stern in search of Lederer Tourneur and his wife, but the only person he found was a young woman who, far removed from all the commotion, was stretched out on a lounge chair with a preoccupied look on her face. Arledge recognized her right away: the black-haired young lady he had seen with Hugh

Everett Bayham. Delighted, he quickly sat down two chairs away from her, though since she was facing the other direction, she did not notice his sly maneuver. Arledge was beside himself with excitement, for this seemed to be the perfect opportunity to make his presence known and to casually insert himself into the pianist's realm, but he was a bit stumped as to how he might properly strike up a conversation, since the troubled voices of the other passengers, vaguely audible from that distance, were a bothersome reminder of the bizarre circumstance in which they found themselves. Chatting about the weather or something similar would seem terribly contrived, he thought, and so he racked his mind for another conversation opener. Given that they were still complete strangers, he felt it would be in bad taste to bring up the topic of Collins's death and its many repercussions, and on the other hand, the consternation he had spied on the young lady's face was not obvious enough for him to offer his unconditional support for whatever problem was vexing her. With this in mind, he decided to simply let his metal cigarette case fall from his hands when he removed a cigarette. As she heard it clatter against the floor, the young woman jumped up with a start and Arledge took advantage of the moment to beg her pardon for his clumsiness, and he then apologized for having disturbed her, and introduced himself. The young woman, with her blue eyes and sweet face, in her elegant yet simple clothes, told him it was quite all right, she hadn't been sleeping and was delighted to make his acquaintance: she had read four of his novels and thought them excellent, though she hadn't ever been lucky enough to see any of the celebrated theatrical adaptations of his works because she lived in the country and the theater, she pointed out, was the privilege of the city dweller. Her diction was perfect if slightly affected, though rather than being a shortcoming Arledge found that this idiosyncrasy only made her more enchanting, and her voice was muted and marvelously mellifluous. She was discreet but friendly, which caused Arledge—

who had already abandoned his usual reserved attitude—to forget the reason he had begun speaking to her in the first place, and they soon found themselves immersed in an animated conversation—within, of course, the bounds of what two timid, well-educated people would consider appropriate—regarding the mediocrity of the contemporary theater, the void left by the death of the author of *A Florentine Tragedy* and *The Duchess of Padua,* and the limitations of the actor's craft. Through all this the young lady listened attentively and occasionally contributed some extremely apt observations and critical insights to their debate. For over an hour and a half they spoke undisturbed, and from the theater they ventured onto other topics, and still others, as animatedly as before, until they suddenly heard footsteps approaching and looked up to see an incensed Hugh Everett Bayham calling out to the young woman, whose full name was Florence Bonington. When he reached them, he stopped and apologized for interrupting the conversation, but he had been searching the boat from top to bottom looking for the young woman, because it was time for lunch and her father was waiting for her.

"Oh, the two of you haven't met, have you? Mr. Victor Arledge, Mr. Hugh Everett Bayham."

The two men shook hands and Florence then stood up, expressed her sincere hope that they might resume their conversation at some other time, bid Arledge farewell, and walked off clutching Bayham's arm.

After waiting a few minutes so as to avoid catching up with them, Arledge then turned to walk toward the dining room as well.

For the next few days, Victor Arledge was truly content and his naturally good humor returned. Thanks to Collins's death on one hand and his ice-breaking conversation with Bayham and his young friend on the other, his lethargy dissipated because he finally felt that all those hours of obsession had not been spent in vain. From that date onward, though Arledge might have appeared carefree to the casual observer, his five senses were all on high alert, expectant, waiting to catch the opportunity for another exchange, either with one of his fellow passengers who might have some interesting information to share about Florence and her father, with father and daughter alone, or with Bayham. Without a doubt, the young woman—perhaps for other reasons as well—had come to occupy a prominent place in Arledge's mind, much in the same way that Bayham had inspired his curiosity before, and this, far from being a source of concern, made him feel more alive than ever before. Though unable to identify exactly why he was suddenly so riveted by Florence Bonington, who hadn't really done anything to deserve such attentions, Arledge now hung on her every move and gesture, hoping against hope for a chance at a conversation, a greeting, a smile, a furtive glance. It wasn't long before he realized. Florence Bonington was very young—no more than nineteen—and though she was obviously no fifteen-year-old child, her perfect, slightly icy beauty and her facial features in general did match the description of the talented piano student's sister, the one who had seduced Hugh Everett Bayham. The physical resemblance, then, was what inspired Arledge to woo her and gain her sympathies with whatever methods he could think of. I do not deny that there was some truth to the initial explanation Arledge gave for his interest in the young lady, but I will also add that Esmond Handl's letter, and not the obvious charms of Miss Bonington, also played a part as well. If Arledge, who enjoyed tremendous success with women and never had to work very hard to seduce them, was now taking such great pains to cultivate a friendship with Florence Bonington, it was because on one hand, through Bayham—his principal objective—he had become intrigued by this woman—if in fact she was the woman he suspected she was—and the rapture she was capable of inspiring, and also because on the other hand, he felt certain that she was just the right person who, once she had succumbed to his charms, could tell him all about what had really happened during Bayham's adventure in Scotland, for she would certainly have full knowledge of the facts. And so Arledge anxiously awaited the moment he would finally lay eyes on the young lady's father, who as of yet had not appeared on the deck of the *Tallahassee,* to see if the old man was, as he suspected, a gentleman with silvery temples, arched eyebrows, a straight nose, and an intelligent gaze.

It took Kerrigan and Seebohm three days to sort out the paperwork relating to Collins's death and obtain McLiam's authorization to continue their voyage, and though this brief period was darkened somewhat by the ominous shadow of unknown, ferocious bandits, as well as the possibility that the expedition might be cancelled altogether, the respite on dry land served a valuable purpose, for it restored the passengers' spirits, calmed their anxieties, and relieved the weak stomach of Esmond Handl, who for once felt like his old self again. Alexandria, in addition, turned out to be one of the most astonishing, breathtaking cities the travelers had ever seen, and they strolled through her streets with genuine pleasure. Things seemed to have improved in every sense, and during the time the *Tallahassee* was anchored in the Egyptian port, Arledge no longer felt tempted to end his travels in Tangiers—a change of heart that was perhaps only temporary but quite spectacular indeed.

On one of these three days (specifically, two days before the sailboat was to depart Alexandria), Arledge had taken a lovely long walk through some of the city's most picturesque neighborhoods in the company of the Handls. When they were finished, the Handls left him alone for a few moments to do a bit of shopping, and so Arledge sat down at a café with an Italian name, intending to order a refreshment and shake off the coat of dust that had settled on his suit, virtually eliminating all the color from it. Just as he did so, he suddenly spied Bayham, Florence Bonington, and a gentleman whose features he couldn't quite distinguish, either trying to communicate or arguing—it was difficult to tell—with a street vendor a short distance away, and so he very quickly ordered a lemonade and told the waiter he would be right back. Summoning what one might call valor—not inaccurately, for his interests were at stake—he went over to the group, where Bayham was gesticulating to the street vendor. Arledge assumed he was watching a rather unsuccessful attempt at bargaining.

"Good day," he said, turning to Florence Bonington. "You seem to be having trouble with this expert salesman. If you'd like, I'd be glad to step in as your interpreter."

"Oh, good day, Mr. Arledge," said the young woman, smiling at him. The stocky, vulgar, and badly dressed man standing beside her did the same, as his daughter added, "I don't believe you've met my father, have you? Mr. Arledge, I'd like to introduce you to my father, Dr. Bonington."

"How do you do," said the novelist, unable to conceal the disappointment that flashed across his face. Dr. Bonington acknowledged the greeting with a slight nod of the head.

"It seems that this salesman is trying to cheat us, Mr. Arledge, and Hugh, as you can tell, does not seem able to communicate with him," said Florence, lightly tapping Bayham on the shoulder as he attempted to count out a price on his fingers, oblivious to Arledge's presence. After a moment, Bayham turned around, politely said hello to Arledge, and explained his predicament.

"This man wants three pounds for this vase. I think three pounds is far too expensive, and I am trying to make him understand that."

"What would you say is a fair price?"

"One pound and a half, for example."

"I'm afraid that you will have a devil of a time trying to communicate such a number with your fingers, Mr. Bayham."

"Well, I don't mind paying three pounds for something I admire, even if it isn't worth it," declared Florence Bonington. "But all the same it bothers me that he is trying to cheat us."

"Don't you worry, Miss Bonington," replied Arledge. "I think I can help you."

Turning to the vendor, Arledge explained the situation in his acceptable, if limited, Arabic. A pound and a half was a terribly low price, said the vendor, but in the end he agreed, and Arledge handed him the money. With the vase in his hands, he turned to Florence and said, "Miss Bonington, please accept this as a gift from me."

"My goodness, thank you, Mr. Arledge, but it's really not necessary…"

"Please. Not another word. And now, do allow me to treat you to a refreshment at that café right over there. I won't take no for an answer. I have a table and a lemonade that was ice-cold just a few moments ago waiting for me. Please."

Dr. Bonington seemed hesitant, but Bayham interceded.

"We wouldn't dream of refusing you, Mr. Arledge. We would be delighted to join you."

"Alexandria is such a lovely city," said Florence, once they were sitting comfortably at their table. "I do believe I could be happy living here."

"It might be a bit uncomfortable," replied Arledge. "There is such a mix of races and nationalities here, and that never makes for a very tranquil environment in which to live. All those clashing temperaments flare up, creating all sorts of trouble all the time."

"But don't forget, Mr. Arledge," Bayham replied, "now that France has relinquished control to Britain, things can only improve."

"Perhaps, but it is still quite unsafe here. In addition to this potpourri of races and faces, the city is full of sailors from all over the world who are all too pleased to give full rein to their barbaric instincts. A port city is twice as dangerous as any other. As for me, I assure you that I wouldn't dream of coming here at nine in the evening."

"Oh, I do think you're exaggerating a bit, Mr. Arledge, not to mention that you're spoiling our plans! We were thinking of taking a stroll in town this evening," said Florence. "I understand the sunset is spectacular."

"Well, I certainly didn't mean to, but I do think I should warn you that this is a rather dangerous place. I don't find the level of police protection here at all satisfactory, and I can assure you it would be nothing short of suicide to walk through the harbor area at that hour. The area is just teeming with professional thieves and to tell the truth, I would say that any resident of Alexandria is a potential assailant. Consider that salesman you just fought off. If he had been a bit younger he would have robbed us of everything we had; we were fortunate he only tried to cheat us out of a few extra shillings, and not very insistently at that."

"I still think you're exaggerating, Mr. Arledge," Bayham replied. "Yes, of course there is some level of danger here, but no more than in any other large city."

"Like London, for example?"

"Why, yes—London is a city that I would not call entirely safe."

"I couldn't agree more, Mr. Bayham. I understand you were recently the victim of an assault there."

"Well, I still think Alexandria is a perfectly charming city, no matter what you say," Florence said, quickly interrupting Arledge.

"There is no doubt about that," Arledge replied. "But that doesn't mean that…"

At that very moment, Arledge noticed that Léonide Meffre was walking directly over to the table where he, Bayham, and the Boningtons were sitting.

"Oh, hello, Meffre," Florence's father called out, extending his hand. "Won't you join us?"

Arledge, though unable to hide the scowl of disgust that had suddenly and very involuntarily come across his face, had no other choice but to make room for the French poet, who sat down and said, "I have a message for you, Arledge. I just saw your friends, I don't recall their names... the ones who write the songs."

"The Handls," Arledge retorted brusquely.

"That's right. Well, Mr. Handl was feeling a bit indisposed after such a long walk, so he and his wife returned to the boat. They asked me to find you and give you the message as well as their apologies."

"Thank you very much, Meffre," said the novelist, making an effort to render a tone of voice that matched his polite words. "It seems that Esmond is just never going to be able to enjoy this voyage..."

The group fell silent for a moment and Meffre, somewhat uncomfortable, hurried to fill the void.

"I do apologize for interrupting you. Please, go on with your conversation, I beg of you."

Dr. Bonington ran his hand over his hair and said, "I don't even remember what we were talking about anymore."

Arledge took advantage of the moment to refresh their memory. "We were discussing something rather unpleasant that happened to Mr. Bayham in London a few months ago."

The pianist seemed to react violently to this; Arledge's abrupt change of topic had caught him off guard. Stammering, he said, "Well, in reality I don't think it can quite be called 'unpleasant.' I'd say it was more of an extraordinary circumstance that—"

"Pardon me for interrupting, Hugh," Florence suddenly interjected, pointing at someone not far away, "but isn't that Lambert Littlefield? We've scarcely seen him at all on deck."

Everyone turned to look in the direction Florence had pointed, and together they studied the man in question.

"Oh, no, that's not him," said Bayham. "Littlefield is much taller, much more elegant than that."

"He's very rich, isn't he?"

"That's right—a millionaire, in fact. That's why he writes so much. He doesn't have to do a thing to earn the unfathomable amount of money he pockets every day. That is why he has so much free time to write his novels."

"Have any of you read his book *Louisiana*?"

"No," the four other men responded in unison.

"Oh, it's quite good, but far too squalid for me. The kind of book that makes you think that everyone in New Orleans is a ruthless speculator."

Arledge couldn't resist the temptation to insert a comment, despite the fact that, as Florence was making her observation, he privately acknowledged to himself that his method was proving to be clumsy and inappropriate to his purposes.

"Perhaps New Orleans is more dangerous even than London or Alexandria."

"Very possible," said Meffre. "A friend of mine was attacked four times during the three months he was in New Orleans."

"You were attacked in London, isn't that right, Mr. Bayham?"

"No," replied Bayham.

"What happened to you, then?" the English novelist asked, persistent as ever. Once again, he realized that he had made his interest a bit too obvious. He himself had no idea why he was being so impatient and tactless and, very briefly, a strange idea (which he immediately discarded) flashed through his mind: perhaps, underneath it all, he really didn't want to learn the details of Bayham's story. Perhaps what he really wanted was never to solve that mystery, so that he could simply contemplate it in its unformed and most vexing phase forevermore. He was just getting ready to garnish his question with an extra phrase or two to make it seem a bit more nonchalant when Dr. Bonington began to say something.

"You know, I was attacked once in Leiden."

Nervous and exasperated by now, Arledge sat up in his chair, determined not to let the conversation digress any further. Perhaps he had gotten ahead of himself, interrogating Bayham so directly and insistently when he barely even knew the man, but he also knew that he had been so insensitive precisely because of the tremendous disappointment he had felt when he saw that Dr. Bonington in no way resembled the gentleman from the carriage that had kidnapped Bayham. He had made his irritation very visible, and now he was determined not to let his feelings ruin the very positive progress he had made. But it was too late. Dr. Bonington, in an atmospheric, evocative tone, was now regaling the group with anecdotes from his life as a university student in Leiden, touching on a wide variety of topics, all of them equally trite: he told stories about a cabaret singer, a mysterious older student whose family had begun to disappear one by one (each missing relative had been seen for the last time on April 6 of four successive years), a professor accused of murder, a watchmaker who collected hands, a story of adolescent love, and other such tall tales. Arledge was beginning to think he was never going to be able to coax the story calmly and discreetly out of Bayham, and with silent fury observed Dr. Bonington, who bored him to distraction with his ridiculous stories about the insipid life and times of a frivolous, commonplace medical student. Arledge feared he would never stop talking. It seemed that Léonide Meffre was equally uninspired by Florence's father, because at one point he actually interrupted the old man— Meffre was always so unbelievably rude—to order another glass of beer from the waiter, although he apologized immediately and urged Dr. Bonington to continue talking.

But Dr. Bonington seemed to have taken the hint.

"Oh, don't be concerned, my dear Meffre. My conversation is neither pleasant nor polite and I must be boring you all to tears. By the way, if we plan to eat lunch on the boat we had best start back right away. It's gotten rather late; perhaps you should cancel that last beer."

That was exactly what Meffre did, and Bayham, despite the protests of Arledge and Bonington, paid the bill as the group, in a rather sour mood now, got up to leave, and began walking toward the harbor. Meffre positioned himself next to Florence and her father, who walked ahead of the others, and Arledge fell into step with Bayham. They walked in silence, slightly uncomfortable and unsure of what to say; Arledge kept telling himself that this was a golden opportunity to interrogate Bayham, with no witnesses around, about all that had happened in Scotland, but he couldn't help dwelling on his failed attempts during the conversation at the café and said nothing for a short while. Finally, almost in spite of himself, he plunged back in: "You never did finish telling me about your adventure, Mr. Bayham. Would it be too much to ask you to tell me the rest of the story?"

Bayham stopped cold.

"Mr. Arledge, may I ask why you are so interested?"

"Oh, simple curiosity."

"Simple curiosity? I don't believe it. From the minute we sat down, you have been trying to probe me about it. I would think that by now you might have realized I am not interested in discussing the matter. I thought you a bit more perceptive, sir."

Bayham's response, so straightforward and direct, caught Arledge by surprise, and for a moment he was at a loss for words.

"What I noticed," he managed to say after a few seconds, "is that neither Dr. Bonington nor your daughter wished to discuss it; I did not realize that you felt the same way. Each time you were about to describe what happened, they would interrupt you."

"My good Mr. Arledge, if they interrupted me it was only because they know that I would prefer never to talk about that incident again. They only did it to rescue me from what you—rather tactlessly, I might add—are forcing me to do now. I am sorry, but I cannot respond to your question. I do not wish to discuss it, if you don't mind."

Arledge suddenly felt terribly embarrassed, and as his face turned a deep shade of purple he looked the other way and began to step up his pace. Bayham did the same, wondering if he hadn't been perhaps a bit too harsh with Arledge.

"How did you hear about what happened to me?" he asked, in a kinder tone of voice. "In the papers? The articles that came out in the newspapers were really quite mediocre."

"I found out through Handl," said Arledge.

"Handl? Well, now I really don't understand what has you so interested. Handl was the first person who heard the story—and in fact the only person, in addition to his wife, who heard it directly from me, and… well, you must know the rest."

"I suppose I do," admitted Arledge, somewhat red-faced. "I'm afraid that all of this has been quite unnecessary, most especially since it has made our interactions so fragile and difficult. I believe I owe you an explanation. Please accept my apologies."

"Mr. Arledge, don't give it another thought. Now that we have cleared the air, we can put this matter behind us. Perhaps I should have been a bit more direct with you back at the café; that way we could have avoided this ridiculous conversation entirely. I know I may be exaggerating somewhat, but I truly dislike having to talk about the incident. It brings back some terribly unpleasant memories that I wish never to revisit again."

"Please, sir, you do not need to justify your position. It is I who should apologize to you for having behaved like such a boor. You have my word that I will never bring up the subject again, and now I must ask you to please accept my sincerest apologies and believe me when I say that I truly regret having brought the matter up."

"Well, I myself regret having been so curt with you—most especially you, a writer whose work I admire so much. In a certain sense, Mr. Arledge, I must say I feel flattered that you were so interested in something that happened to me. In that light, your interest is quite a compliment."

"Thank you, Mr. Bayham. I do appreciate your comments. You are a gentleman."

"I hope to think I am."

At that, they quickened their pace until they caught up with the Boningtons and Léonide Meffre, who had already reached the docks. They were still talking about Leiden, or *Louisiana,* or something of the sort. Arledge wasn't certain—you see, he was awfully befuddled by then.

Their last night in Alexandria was a gloomy one. The passengers, conscious that the little vacation they had enjoyed during their extended stopover in the Egyptian city was now coming to an end, and also aware that, having been prompted by a series of factors beyond their control, it would most likely not be repeated, sat around the salon, downcast and glum. Only those passengers planning to disembark for good at Tangiers were in relatively good spirits; for them the end of the voyage was not so far off now. The rest of the expeditioners, including Bayham, the Handls, Florence and Dr. Bonington, Kerrigan, Meffre, and Victor Arledge were all thinking the same thing now: that the premise for the trip had been incredibly flimsy to begin with, and that the expedition may very well have been doomed from the start, and now more than ever they began to wish with all their heart that the *Tallahassee* would suddenly succumb to a technical problem so dire that the vessel would be unable to complete the ambitious voyage. Had just one of the passengers—just one—dared to voice these doubts and misgivings, it is highly likely that the rest of the passengers would have seconded the opinion and insisted that the boat immediately turn back to Marseilles, but everyone was so unsure of how their fellow travelers would react to such a suggestion that they all kept their mouths shut, and the following day the boat set off once again, leaving behind not only a place that everyone, in those odd circumstances, had grown terribly fond of, but also the only two things that had made the trip at all intriguing for Victor Arledge: the death of Collins, the boatswain, and the hope of finding out, some day, something about the unusual adventures of Hugh Everett Bayham. The carriage, the kidnappers, the music, the house by the sea, the captivity, and the jealousy and rancor of the three sisters would never be explained to him.

For six days, the *Tallahassee* traveled swiftly and serenely along the North African coastline, without anything unusual happening on board. Aside from the vague feeling of disappointment that had come over the expeditioners as they saw the first part of their voyage come to a close, the suffocating heat sapped them of whatever energy they might have otherwise possessed to voice their very lukewarm desires regarding possible ports of call or the general administration of the sailing vessel. The ladies, overcome by fatigue, let their fans fall to the ground, and the men either holed up in their staterooms or played games of chess and cards, with their shirts and vests unbuttoned or bare-chested. The irate crew had calmed down by this point and now spent much of its ample leisure time intoning ballads and lewd songs that, after a few hours, became part of the eternal hum of life onboard the boat. The scientists, ignored by their fellow passengers from the very beginning, wore themselves out trying to execute calculations that would justify their presence on the boat. Huddled together in Captain Seebohm's quarters, they grew dizzy and disoriented from the heat. Kerrigan, having left his business in the hands of some negligent underling, mourned the death of three of his Manchurian ponies and, disconsolate and anguished, gulped down one drink after the other, resting on an ottoman at the bar of the smoking lounge which, for some reason, he had taken to calling a "stinking whorehouse."

Things went on like this until one night, as the *Tallahassee* sailed away from the Tunisian ports and the majority of the people who had once dreamed of being adventurers convened in the brightly lit salon, Lederer Tourneur, glancing at the headlines of a newspaper a waiter had just brought him, sat up and exclaimed: "My goodness, what a dreadful story!"

At that, the atmosphere on board perked up considerably.

"What is it?" asked Amanda Cook, the cellist, visibly alarmed by the English short-story writer's sudden outburst.

Tourneur paid no attention to the lady's question, and simply continued reading the news article, slowly and occasionally sucking in his breath, incredulous, as she, fidgety and nervous as always, searched the eyes of the other people in the room, hoping to hear the answer that, obviously, only Tourneur could provide.

"It seems that Mr. Tourneur has discovered something," Léonide Meffre whispered into Amanda Cook's ear, though not so softly that the others couldn't hear him.

"This is terrible, perfectly terrible..." Tourneur murmured to himself as his eyes scanned the columns of the front page. "When will they put an end to all this?"

"Excuse me for interrupting your reading, Mr. Tourneur," said Lambert Littlefield, the wealthy and celebrated author of *Louisiana,* not to mention the only American on board the *Tallahassee* aside from Kerrigan and Marjorie Tourneur, "but we would all be very interested to know what has happened to so gravely alter the tone of your voice."

Tourneur looked up from the newspaper and stared back at the expectant crowd that now faced him. Some of the men, including Bayham and Dr. Bonington, who were sitting at a table close to the sofas occupied by Littlefield and Tourneur, had been playing cards but suspended their game momentarily to move closer to the circle, their curiosity awakened by the exclamations of Tourneur, who responded somberly: "Ladies and gentlemen, it appears that Raisuli has kidnapped another man and a child."

"Raisuli?" Florence Bonington exclaimed. "Who is Raisuli?"

"Didn't you read about him in the newspapers, about a month

ago?" Meffre asked impatiently. "He kidnapped Walter Harris, a correspondent for the London *Times*. While they were negotiating his release Raisuli went off and kidnapped two more people. It was quite astonishing!"

"I never read the newspaper," Florence remarked. "Who is Raisuli?"

"Whom did he kidnap this time?" asked Meffre at the same time, trying to show off a bit.

"An American citizen and his stepson," replied Tourneur. "Now, listen to this, Mr. Littlefield, his name is Ion Perdicaris. You wouldn't know anything about him, would you?"

"No, I've never heard the name before in my life—and quite an extravagant name at that, I'd say. Doesn't the newspaper say anything?"

"All it says is that the victims are American citizens. It seems your people are in the same boat as we are now, eh, Mr. Little-field?"

"Well, I'm afraid that my government will be asking your government to coordinate their rescue. If there is any representative, even only semiofficial, of the Western world in Morocco, it would be Great Britain."

"Ah," Esmond Handl piped up, "I regret to inform you that within a few days there will be an exchange of powers, and England will cede control of this region to France in exchange for total freedom of operation in Egypt. Mr. Littlefield's government will have to pay, and your government, Meffre, will have to carry out the negotiations with the kidnappers."

"I disagree," said Meffre. "The kidnapping occurred today, and not 'within a few days,' which means that the responsibility falls to the British. Morocco needs to be run with an iron fist, and that is just what France will use. In a few days, just as you say, I am sure things will have improved measurably and all this madness will come to an end."

"Where were—Perdicaris, was that his name? Where were he and his son kidnapped?" Littlefield inquired.

"In Tangiers, in broad daylight," replied Tourneur. "What a disgrace. To kidnap a child is really the most abominable thing…"

"Please," said Florence Bonington, "I think I am beginning to get a picture of what you are talking about, but won't someone be kind enough to explain to me who this Raisuli is? I apologize for being so ignorant."

"I've no idea who he is either, darling," said Marjorie Tourneur, placing an affectionate hand on Florence's arm.

Victor Arledge saw that Bayham was about to respond to Miss Bonington, and quickly interceded before Bayham could say anything: "Ahmed Ben Mohammed Raisuli is a local Berber chief— a strongman, as they say. The people are up in arms because the sultan Abdul Aziz is trying to introduce certain European customs in the country. The Berber tribes have rebelled against this, and have taken advantage of the widespread dissatisfaction among their compatriots, who help them and hide them when necessary, in their settlements along the Algerian border. Raisuli kidnapped Walter Harris and asked for an exorbitant amount of ransom money; I imagine he'll do the same with Perdicaris."

"There's one thing you've left out, Mr. Arledge," Meffre said. "They plan to buy weapons with their ransom money."

"Weapons? Are they staging a revolution?" asked Amanda Cook.

"An insurrection," said Littlefield.

"But that would compromise our interests there, wouldn't it?"

"Yes, precisely. This is a terribly critical moment."

"They would be wise to evacuate the entire British civilian population there," Handl observed.

"Do you really believe it's that dangerous?" asked Florence. "That imminent?"

"You never know, Miss Bonington. If the lives of those two

men and that child can be saved by paying up, it is quite likely that the Berbers will attempt to take Melilla with the weapons they buy with their ransom money, and that would indeed be a very tricky problem to solve."

"They shouldn't pay the ransom, then," Meffre stated categorically.

"Well, that is a rather delicate question," Bayham said. "The lives of three innocent people are at stake here. I hardly think you should speak so lightly, sir."

"I have a question…" Clara Handl began to say.

"I am not speaking lightly, Mr. Bayham; be assured of that. I rarely do," stated Meffre.

"True enough," Arledge noted.

"I want to know if we are going to be in any danger."

"Your irony, Mr. Arledge, is out of line."

"There was no irony in my observation, Mr. Meffre. You never speak lightly about anything, although perhaps you did just now, if only to contradict what I said."

"Arledge, I must warn you that I will not tolerate your impertinence for one more second."

"Sir, the only impertinent person here is you. I have simply seconded a statement that you yourself made. What more do you want from me?"

"I was speaking with Mr. Bayham, not with you, sir. Intervening in a private conversation is something I consider impertinent."

"A private conversation in the company of a dozen other people? You know, I believe Mr. Bayham was right: you shouldn't speak so lightly about such a thing, Mr. Meffre, but if you do, you should learn how to do it with a bit more tact."

"You insult me, sir!"

"That is not my intention. I assure you that if I had truly wanted to insult you, your face would be quite red by now."

"Gentlemen, please be reasonable about things," said Little-field. "We were discussing a very serious matter."

"That is correct: the lives of three people," observed Arledge, who always liked to have the last word. He then looked up at Hugh Everett Bayham, who flashed him a complicit, grateful smile. As Dr. Bonington cast aspersions on the character of Raisuli in an effort to ease the tension that now gripped the room, Little-field, Tourneur, and Handl attacked the sultan's excessive caution, for without his consent the British troops were unable to do any-thing at a time when they were keen to teach the rebels a lesson once and for all. Arledge, meanwhile, mused over how Léonide Meffre's ridiculous though not unwarranted touchiness had al-lowed him to establish a kind of complicity with Bayham, which no doubt would mellow into friendship: the kind that inspires tac-tical alliances and shared impunity. His hopes of finding out what had happened in Scotland, which had vanished (at least, that is what he thought at the time: that they had vanished practically without a fight) when they departed Alexandria, came back with a vengeance as they left Tunisia.

The *Tallahassee* sailed on, its lights visible from the shore.

On that sailboat absolutely nothing was predictable, and no matter how irrevocable a decision seemed, no matter how despi-cably someone may have behaved, the simple suggestion that things might take a turn for the better had a way of making the passengers—in a way that was always unexpected and never fully appreciated at first or at the most difficult moments, despite abun-dant evidence to the effect—eventually see things that had once discouraged them in a new, positive, and promising light, as prom-ising as everything had seemed the day that the *Tallahassee* had set sail from Marseilles. When this uncanny phenomenon materialized with power and force, through the front page of the newspaper, a feeling of glee and high spirits came over the passengers, especial-ly the novelist Victor Arledge. What was it, then, that led Victor

Arledge to make the unusual decision to abandon all his fear, tact, caution, and prudence, and risk his reputation to find out the reason Hugh Everett Bayham had been kidnapped and taken to Scotland and the identity of the young woman who had charmed him so? Was it the potent energy on the *Tallahassee*—energy that was, of course, ephemeral, unsustainable, and undermined by constant setbacks? Or was it his desperate need to shatter the tension produced by the constantly changing objectives and his own inability to identify even one thing to cling to that was solid and stable? Nobody would ever know for sure, and as time went by it would become terribly important, because it was a decision that eventually led to the great writer's disappearance, reclusion, apathy, surrender, and death, under circumstances that, while perhaps not wretched, were probably not the kind of circumstances that any artist, or anyone who aspires to immortality, would have willingly chosen for himself.

BOOK FOUR

As I waited for Mr. Branshaw to continue during a very long pause, I found myself studying the designs on the rug when I suddenly heard the sound of the book slam shut. I lifted my head, startled by the noise, which I hadn't been expecting, and watched as Miss Bunnage, whose general attitude seemed to corroborate my hunch that the reading had come to an end, dutifully placed the cap on her fountain pen and carefully, methodically stored the pages upon which she, almost continuously since Mr. Branshaw had begun to read, had been furiously scribbling her impressions of *Voyage Along the Horizon,* though perhaps she had been writing about some other topic of interest; I cannot be sure, for when the sound of the pen scratching against the paper distracted me enough to try to decipher what she was writing—from a bit of a distance—Miss Bunnage's tiny and rather irregular penmanship, at least from my position, was illegible and as such, I may have had a reasonable idea of what she was writing but I could not ascertain anything for certain. And while I realize that my maneuver may have suggested immaturity and a sore lack of investigative talents on my part, I must admit that for a few mo-

ments I didn't know what to think: though it had taken Mr.
Holden Branshaw the entire morning to read it, the text was not
very long at all—perhaps some eighty pages—and as such, not
substantial enough to be a complete novel, not even the shortest
novel, given the thickness of the volume from which he read. But
at the same time I was also able to imagine, from the tone and
mood of the last paragraph, that the author might have intended
an open ending, the kind without any real conclusion, and since
our host had mentioned the previous evening that his friend had
never quite ascertained why Victor Arledge had decided to retire
from the world, I was not sure whether to voice an opinion of
some sort or ask how many chapters remained to be read. When
I finally decided to open my mouth, more than anything to break
the embarrassing silence observed by both Miss Bunnage, who was
busy gathering up her professional tools, and Branshaw, who stared
at us impassively, waiting for some kind of comment, the only
thing I could think of to say, partially to appease my host, who
made his impatience all too obvious as he drummed his fingers
over and over again on the cover of the book, was that the novel
was truly fascinating despite the fact that the story was a bit
cumbersome and the dialogues often quite inferior to the narrative. Branshaw seemed displeased with this assessment, and said
nothing for a few moments, making me fear that when he opened
his mouth anew it would only be to expel us from his home without further ado, so hostile was the expression that came over his
face following my innocent observation, which I had actually
thought complimentary. But when he finally broke his silence, it
was merely to express his very sincere desire that we resume the
reading at another time—perhaps the following morning because,
as he noted, he was feeling a bit too tired to keep on reading out
loud in a clear voice—which was absolutely necessary—and in
any event, after lunch he had a number of pressing appointments
which had been scheduled several days before we had all agreed to

gather at his house for the reading. Miss Bunnage, far more clever than I (right then, I realized that she had responded so rapidly when Branshaw had closed the book because she had correctly understood his gesture to mean not closure but rather a brief respite), veritably lunged toward the front door of the house and thanked Mr. Branshaw and bid him farewell until the following day. Then she turned to me and very clearly hinted that I ought to escort her home, and I responded, not without a bit of a blush creeping up my cheeks, that I would be happy to oblige.

As we walked out, Miss Bunnage was lively and light-footed, almost like a Manchurian pony trotting down the street, whereas I, not entirely satisfied with how things had evolved since my party the previous evening, simply offered her my arm.

When we arrived at her house, a low building with a white façade, green doors and shutters, old-fashioned simplicity, and a welcoming ambience, Miss Bunnage invited me to stay for lunch, and though I demurred at first she insisted so strenuously that I had no choice but to give in, albeit somewhat grudgingly. It seemed that she lived alone with a matronly servant woman who grumbled as she came out to greet us, and her fortune, which appeared to be inherited, must have been quite considerable, judging by the paintings on the walls and the quality of the furniture that decorated the rooms. After leading me into a spacious dining room, Miss Bunnage asked me if I would care for an aperitif. She left the room to fulfill my request—despite the fact that I had worked up quite an appetite and wanted to avoid whetting it any further, I knew I couldn't possibly bear another round of effusive entreaties and solicitous insistence—and then, as I took tiny sips of sack, she and the servant woman set the table for two.

The first course left much to be desired, and the prolonged stretches of silence that followed Miss Bunnage's many vague and terribly boring inquiries regarding my person were intolerable; but by the time we reached the second course, I became aware that the

JAVIER MARÍAS

situation was not going to improve unless I wanted it to and, uninterested in provoking any more excessive and unnecessary excitement or irritation, I decided to introduce a new topic of conversation, one that held little or no interest for me at the time: the novel *Voyage Along the Horizon*. I did this in the hope of coaxing back Miss Bunnage's smile, which had disappeared and been replaced by a rather stubborn grimace of surly disenchantment. Contrary to what I had assumed, as the title of the work fell from my lips, Miss Bunnage jumped slightly in her chair and her face grew even more somber. Surprised by her reaction, I stopped talking for a few moments, to give her time to regain her composure, and once she had calmed down a bit, with the aid of a napkin, which she used to hide her chagrined face as she pulled herself together, I repeated my interest in the topic, not because I wanted to cause her any more distress—nothing could have been further from my intentions—but because I did not want her to realize that I had perceived her distress upon hearing the title of the novel written by Mr. Branshaw's dead friend.

And in effect, my tactic worked: this time, Miss Bunnage, who knew what I was after and was now prepared for anything, smiled at my question (Do you know if Victor Arledge actually participated in the journey described in Mr. Branshaw's manuscript and if the other characters actually existed?), took a bite of her steak, smiled again, enigmatically this time, and said: "You find the story rather mad, don't you? Well, it is, in a sense. But I should warn you that for the moment I cannot tell you very much about it, and I truly apologize, because I do feel that the two of us are now like a pair of comrades-in-arms, and I do feel it is only fair that you should know the truth. But alas, I cannot tell you today; perhaps tomorrow, when Mr. Branshaw has finished reading the entire book. You see, if I were to answer your question now, I would feel like one of those writers who allow people to read their novels before they are finished, and I wouldn't like that one bit, for you would think me an impatient woman who doesn't know how to remain silent when she is supposed to. One must learn how to cultivate the art of ambiguity. So please, do forgive me, and I promise you that tomorrow I will give you a fully convincing, satisfactory explanation that will surely come as a great surprise."

I think it important to mention that when I asked her that question, it was not in the hope of actually eliciting a response that would satisfy my curiosity, because I felt no curiosity, and for precisely that reason I found Miss Bunnage's long-winded reply rather perplexing: on one hand she did not confirm whether the events described in *Voyage Along the Horizon* had actually occurred—now that I had asked her, why not find out the truth?—and on the other hand, when I least expected it, she introduced a whole new series of enigmas in my mind that, perhaps not right then but certainly at some point later on—an idle moment when I had nothing better or more interesting to think about, for example—I might find quite troubling. The shock must have been quite visible on my face, and Miss Bunnage, perhaps perceiving my incipient and now uneasy interest, appreciated it tremendously, and so now with no desire whatsoever to continue down this path of conversation, I simply said: "Of course!"

The rest of the meal went by uneventfully, and the conversation was even rather trivial, but by the time I had left Miss Bunnage's house, my opinion of her had changed considerably. Now, of course, I cannot help but think of her with more than mere affection, and though I met her but two times in my life, her fragile figure, which she so innocently tried to infuse with airs of mystery even though there was no way she could ever hide her innate goodness, has become meaningful to me in a way that even now I am unable to describe fully. We never did return to the topic of the novel by Mr. Branshaw's friend, and once we had moved past the tense interchange at the beginning of our luncheon, we found plenty of things—banal but entertaining—to talk about, and time

passed quite rapidly as we drank our tea and watched the sun go
down. During those three or four hours I spent at her house on
Finsbury Road, I discovered Miss Bunnage, ambiguously but most
certainly in the autumn of her life, to be far more intelligent than
I had originally presumed, and perhaps this newfound appreciation
was what caused my interest in *Voyage Along the Horizon,* at first
passive, then indifferent, grow more acute—more than anything, I
am afraid, because of the fondness and admiration that, little by little, Miss Bunnage's opinions had inspired in me, to the extent that
when we parted that afternoon, planning to reconvene the following day, I came terribly close to reminding her of the promise she
had made to me, but then decided against it, feeling it would be
inappropriate, and so I said nothing, leaving myself at the mercy of
her wishes, her whims, her feelings, her will, and fate itself.

The following day, Mr. Branshaw received me, frosty but courteous as usual, and insisted I enjoy a drink with him as we awaited
the arrival of Miss Bunnage, who appeared to be running late. Mr.
Branshaw and I passed the time drinking Italian wine and exchanging a bit of bland conversation. He seemed so very listless
that I had to wonder what on earth had made his friend so special
that, upon his death, Branshaw would feel so compelled to cham-
pion his only novel, proclaim its excellence, and play a role that, in
theory, required an enthusiasm he so sorely lacked. Something of
a cross between an executor and a biographer, Mr. Branshaw really did not possess the qualifications for either role, and on one
hand, while he did not seem to be overflowing with joy at the
prospect of having to read, to two strangers, a book that he considered to be the most important novel of his time, he was also not
at all bothered by it either. Whether his icy attitude was real, apparent, or acquired, I had no idea, and under other circumstances I
would have simply said I didn't care, but that day, perhaps as an
extension of the homage I rendered Miss Bunnage with my
curiosity regarding *Voyage Along the Horizon,* I felt a pressing need

to understand his reasons. Averse as I am to prying, however, I chose to remain silent and, with considerable impatience, reminded myself that Miss Bunnage understood the matter at hand and would, sooner or later, keep the promise she had made to me.

Mr. Branshaw, sitting in an easy chair with the novel in his hands, cleared his throat, troubled that Miss Bunnage was so late, and twenty minutes after the appointed hour he proposed that we continue the reading without further ado, claiming that he could not afford to waste any more time on this matter and that if Miss Bunnage hadn't turned up it must have been because she had found the first part of the novel so boring that she couldn't be bothered to sit through the rest of it. I tried suggesting that there was no way this could be true, and I begged him to wait just ten minutes more. He relented, but it was pointless: Miss Bunnage never turned up, and I, wracked with anxiety and fear, ventured to request that we postpone the reading so that I might go to Miss Bunnage's house—she did not answer when we called—to find out what had happened and to return with her as soon as possible, as long as nothing was seriously wrong, of course.

But Mr. Branshaw seemed to have grown tired of us: he made the vaguest allusion to my comment about the novel the day before, and expressed his disapproval of Miss Bunnage's blasé, fickle behavior, adding in a reproachful tone: "My dear sir, I cannot deny that when I saw the enthusiasm and emotion that came over Miss Bunnage when she heard of my friend's novel, I could not help but feel flattered, for it is of utmost importance to me that this work receive the recognition it deserves, and while I may have originally wished to keep the content of this novel a secret until its publication, I later decided that satisfying the curiosity of Miss Bunnage, such a renowned authority on Victor Arledge, was certainly a worthy pursuit, and in addition, I thought that Miss Bunnage's familiarity with and approval of the text might serve as an ideal launching point for its literary debut. For that reason, though it was nonetheless not an easy decision, I accepted her proposal. As you may have already guessed—and I apologize if this comes as a disappointment—you were invited along simply as a matter of basic courtesy. But now I realize that I committed a grave mistake. Unfortunately, I am now afraid, as I already mentioned, that Miss Bunnage as well must have found the tale rather cumbersome and the dialogue poor, and that it was simply was not worth the effort to come here this morning—and this, no doubt, will be a terrible blow for the future of *Voyage Along the Horizon,* far more disappointing than anything I might have imagined. Please, do not try to convince me otherwise. There is no other plausible explanation for her absence, and most important, I see no reason for us to uselessly prolong this charade, which is deeply painful to me. I do, however, like to think of myself as a fair man, and I do appreciate your... shall we say 'relative' interest in something that was a complete anathema to you until very recently. For that reason, and to put an end to this situation once and for all, I shall read you the rest of the novel, for I do believe that if you took the trouble to come here today and yesterday, it must be out of more than mere courtesy, and your gesture deserves to be reciprocated in the appropriate manner. Please—not another word, I beg of you. Simply listen—that is, if you don't find it a waste of your time, of course."

Intimidated by his speech, which sounded self-effacing yet arrogant at the same time, I nodded my head in grateful acceptance of his offer and, though I was still troubled by the inexplicable absence of Miss Bunnage, I settled down into an easy chair, somewhat overwhelmed, somewhat embarrassed, but also filled with anticipation. Holden Branshaw then opened the tome, announced Book Two, and looked in my eyes for approbation. I smiled and murmured that I was ready to continue our reading, but before I could even finish my sentence he had already picked up where he had left off the day before:

Captain J. D. Kerrigan, who had deferred his authority on board the *Tallahassee* to Captain Eustace Seebohm, an Englishman, in the interest of avoiding bureaucratic difficulties, was perhaps the only person on the sailboat whose mood did not visibly change upon hearing the news about the kidnapping of Ion Perdicaris and his son. Now, Kerrigan may have been drinking excessively before hearing the news of the kidnapping, for he had been devastated by the death of three of his Manchurian ponies, but after hearing the news he increased his alcohol consumption to such a degree that the reserves of whisky stored by the scientists and researchers in the *Tallahassee*'s pantry for exclusively medicinal purposes were depleted to a bare minimum, and to make the situation even worse, Kerrigan soon found himself lamenting the death of four more ponies. The Perdicaris kidnapping, however, wasn't the cause of Kerrigan's mood swings: his sadness and despair were growing increasingly more acute and evident on their own, and his apathy and sorrow deepened by the day. For those who knew him well—to the extent that anyone could "know" a man like Captain J. D. Kerrigan—his very visible decline was not an unfamiliar scenario, and they all knew that the only solution was simply to let things take their course. This circumstance, however, sparked a whole new series of conflicts on board that, had they not involved Kerrigan, might have actually amused Victor Arledge and helped buoy his spirits.

Captain Seebohm, a good-natured man with plenty of seafaring experience, took Kerrigan's crisis in stride at first, believing it to be a simple outburst that was not at all atypical among sailors. This very mistaken conclusion, which he may have reached precisely because of his very extensive experience and tolerant character, eventually drove Seebohm himself into a fit of rage when Kerrigan's excesses began to take on colossal proportions: his presence on the boat had become all but untenable for the passengers and his behavior was setting a truly dismal example for his crew. Kerrigan's obstreperous comportment reached its nadir two days after the passengers on the *Tallahassee* learned of Raisuli's latest exploits: after locking himself up in his cabin for over twenty-four hours with five bottles of whisky, he decided to end his self-imposed confinement only to search for more alcohol, and upon discovering that the pantry doors were locked—on Captain Seebohm's orders—and guarded by a pair of arrogant sailors, who appeared deaf to his demands and offensive language, he barked out sharp words of protest as he stormed off, teetering wildly from side to side despite his efforts to walk as purposefully as possible toward the quarters of his superior. In the middle of this rampage, he bumped right into Amanda Cook, who was semireclined on a lounge chair, and fell to the floor. The cellist, frightened and concerned, rose to her feet immediately and offered to help Kerrigan get back on his feet, apologizing profusely all the while. Kerrigan, incensed and choleric, bolted up, grabbed Amanda Cook by the waist, lifted her up over his head, and threw her overboard, to the horror—yes, horror was what prevailed over any and all other nobler emotions just then—of the other passengers watching on in the vicinity. Several crew members dove into the water after her, but Kerrigan, who seemed to feel that this impulsive action was somehow the key to the solution that would unlock the door to the pantry, lunged at Florence Bonington who stood, paralyzed with terror, between the lounge chair that Amanda Cook had just vacated and the one still occupied by Hugh Everett Bayham. Taking her into his arms, he lifted her up as if she were no heavier than a feather and, holding her high in the air, threatened to deliver her the same fate if he were not given immediate access to the pantry and its contents. Startled by the commotion that erupted when Kerrigan threw Amanda Cook overboard, the people who until then had been scattered randomly about the deck now stood in a cluster in front of Kerrigan, among them Captain Seebohm and Victor Arledge, whose mouths hung open in shock as they contemplated the sight of Miss Bonington held aloft in midair by the second in command, who seemed to have lost his mind. To complicate things, Kerrigan stood with his back to the railing, which made it impossible to subdue him from behind, and a group of crew members, very well built men indeed, were closing in on him from either side but seemed hesitant about making a definitive move to overpower him, possibly fearing that their superior would do just what he had done with Miss Cook, despite the fact that six or seven other men, equally strong, were already poised and ready to jump into the water if Miss Bonington were to fall in, accidentally or otherwise—even though, of course, the idea of a coincidental slip or stumble seemed highly unlikely given the circumstances. As the majority of the ship's passengers stood perfectly still, transfixed by this astonishing scenario, the men who had jumped into the water after Amanda Cook had rescued her by now and were climbing up a ladder on the side of the boat with the cellist over their shoulders, since the *Tallahassee* had come to a complete halt the minute someone had shouted that a woman had fallen overboard and the impromptu lifeguards had proven themselves quite efficient indeed. Kerrigan, however, continued swearing that he would make good on his threat if his demands were not met immediately, and Miss Bonington, by now recovered from the initial shock, only let out a few occasional cries of fatigue and pain. Seebohm and Bayham, who were standing the closest to him, began to move as if they were preparing to pounce on Kerrigan who, upon realizing this, and with an almost inconceivable speed for such a drunken man, responded by moving his arms as if he was indeed going to throw Florence Bonington overboard. Finally, a voice rang out on deck: it was Victor Arledge, whose words rose high above all the whispers as he turned to speak to Kerrigan in a measured, conciliatory tone. Now, to tell the truth, anyone could have come up with the arguments that Arledge used on Kerrigan, but not just anyone could have delivered them quite the way Arledge did. He spoke slowly, with neither hostility nor fear, though in a slightly paternal tone of voice, and little by little Kerrigan began to calm down and his breathing normalized until finally he lowered his arms and, almost delicately, placed Florence Bonington on the deck. Seebohm and his thugs took advantage of the moment to pounce on Kerrigan, who immediately realized he was being attacked and turned on them with a vengeful, fierce look in his eyes. Amid violent shoves and flying fists, he pulled a penknife from his pocket and buried it in the belly—or very close to it—of Captain Eustace Seebohm, who cried out with a squawk similar to those made by doves chasing one another in the air. The blood began to spurt, and the captain of the *Tallahassee* soon fell to the ground. The crew, completely horrified by now, had a very hard time subduing the second in command.

After a few hours, the doctors categorized the knife wound, which had seemed fatal at first, as critical, and declared that Captain Seebohm, whom the rest of the passengers had assumed was dead the moment his bloody body hit the deck, would be out of danger after a day and a half, and despite the fact that his condition would remain critical, the doctors predicted a rapid recovery, barring any unforeseen changes of course. Captain Kerrigan, who took no time at all to recover from his many scrapes and bruises as well as a superficial gash on the head, was immediately apprehended, locked up in his cabin, and placed under tight surveillance, as Fordington-Lewthwaite, the inept officer who would step into the role of ship's captain now that both the first and the second in command were incapacitated, advised the feverish Captain Seebohm—who gave him his consent—to open a case file on Kerrigan for a possible trial which could be held when the *Tallahassee* next dropped anchor at a port under British jurisdiction.

The reasons for Kerrigan's conduct mystified and intrigued all the passengers, with the exception of Victor Arledge and Léonide Meffre who, having been acquainted—in very different ways, but acquainted just the same—with the enigmatic American for some time, knew that it would be absolutely useless to ask him to explain his actions; they knew that such an approach would get them nowhere. No doubt this was why Arledge and Meffre were the only travelers who, beyond the mild consternation that anyone would feel following such an incident, did not seem excessively affected by what had happened, and they simply turned their attentions back to whatever they had been doing before the outburst, amid the ice-cold atmosphere among the other, more anguished passengers and the increasingly hostile crew members who, emboldened by the timid, schoolmarmish ways of Fordington-Lewthwaite, quickly began staging acts of insubordination that would only grow more frequent and daring as time went by. The incident, of course, left everyone stunned: Florence Bonington (who certainly had just cause), Dr. Bonington, Hugh Everett Bayham, the Handls, the Tourneurs, and of course Amanda Cook and the very humanitarian Mr. Littlefield. The mood among them, fragile and once again buffeted by the whims of fate, took a turn for the worse, and their attitude and behavior ever since then have only confirmed my conviction that water was far from the only thing that made things shift and sway and rock wildly aboard the *Tallahassee*. From that day onward, the upper deck was almost always deserted, as the passengers made an effort to fraternize only in the salons, which offered them safety and shelter; only the most intrepid traveler with the most desperate need to feel the warmth of the sun or the evening breeze dared to pop out onto the upper deck every so often and head toward the lounge chairs at the stern, and when he did, he went well armed with cards, liquor, or tobacco to fill those solitary moments out in the fresh air. Among these adventurous types were Victor Arledge, Léonide Meffre, and, once he had recovered from the fright of seeing the woman who could very well be his future wife in the arms of a madman, Hugh Everett Bayham, the rising piano star. Up until this point, however, the three gentlemen had not maintained very cordial relations: Arledge and Meffre ignored, if not despised one another outright; Bayham and Arledge had shared a few rather infelicitous encounters and now kept their distance from each other; and Meffre and the pianist had met, but with rather unpleasant consequences, two years earlier at Baden-Baden. Their interaction had been somewhat circumstantial, and even though the slight friction that had erupted between them in Germany during a performance of Monteverdi's *Ulysses,* involving some box seats and a certain young lady, was more or less ancient history by now, both men (Meffre in particular) still seemed to remain slightly, quietly hesitant about initiating any kind of direct conversation even when the occasion all but required it.

It was for this reason that the three men, brilliant as they all were, fell silent the first few times they bumped into one another by the lounge chairs on the upper deck. Bayham, an inveterate card player, could not bring himself to suggest a friendly round of cards and spent his time playing solitaire instead; Meffre's activities consisted exclusively of smoking a smelly pipe and reading, from top to bottom, every last newspaper that had come his way. Arledge, on the other hand, simply laced his hands together and contemplated the sea, waiting for one of the other men to say something or for Léonide Meffre to disappear from the scene altogether, so that he might summon the necessary courage to start peppering the English pianist with his unseemly questions once again.

Things stayed this way for a while longer than everyone might have expected: nothing out of the ordinary occurred over the next few days, nothing at all that might have been able to boost the passengers' brooding spirits a bit, and so the collective mood onboard only grew darker. With each passing day they clung tighter and tighter to the shelter of their cabins, sick and tired of the voyage even though they didn't fully realize it, blinded as they were by their own apathy. Bored and enervated, they all but forgot what they were doing on the boat in the first place. Everyone was acutely aware of Kerrigan's absence, precisely because he had been such a ubiquitous figure on the boat until then, even during his moments of crisis—charging up and down the deck, looking after every last detail, constantly checking up on the health of his Manchurian ponies, supervising the crew's activities. Somehow Kerrigan had managed to fix things so that the harmony aboard the *Tallahassee* depended entirely on him, and to make things even worse, Fordington-Lewthwaite's ineptitude knew no bounds.

After a few failed attempts, Victor Arledge finally managed to convince Fordington-Lewthwaite to allow him to visit Kerrigan in his cabin, though only after he had been able to ascertain that the British novelist would not be risking his safety by doing so. According to the guards standing watch over him, Kerrigan had still not gotten over his terrible melancholic fit, and spent his days lying in bed, restless and fitful, though he was slightly more serene now that they had gotten him off the alcohol and back onto a regular diet, which led them to believe that he was vastly improved, both physically and mentally.

Kerrigan was asleep when Arledge entered his cabin. As the writer's hand came to rest on his shoulder, Kerrigan jumped up with a start, but when he recognized whom it belonged to, his face broke into a grateful smile. Arledge embraced him tightly, murmured a few encouraging words, and sat down at the foot of the bed, urging Kerrigan to lie back down. He then asked the captain how he was feeling and if he knew what Fordington-Lewthwaite and Seebohm were planning to do about him. In a rather dismissive tone of voice, Kerrigan replied that yes, he knew, but that he was far more concerned about what Arledge thought of his behav-

ior the evening he had stabbed Seebohm and endangered the lives
of the two women. His recollection of it all was extremely hazy.

"Abominable, absolutely abominable," said Arledge, as a con-
spiratorial smile came across his face.

Once he realized that Arledge had not come to his cabin with
recriminations, Kerrigan breathed a sigh of relief and smiled more
easily and confidently, although it was clear that he was still somewhat nervous. Leaning back down on the bed, he rubbed his arms,
perhaps because he was cold, perhaps as a prelude to the conversation he knew they were about to have, perhaps because Arledge's
reply, though friendly, had reminded him of the very embarrassing
situation he now found himself in. Arledge, to calm his nerves a
bit, said, "Listen, what's done is done, it doesn't matter. At least not
to me."

"But it does to me," Kerrigan replied and then, as if this simple
reply had suddenly given him the perfect beginning for a story, he
began to explain, choked up and slightly incoherent, the reasons
he had acted in such a barbaric manner that day.

Victor Arledge had always been a staunch enemy of close
friendship and everything that went along with it, but more important right then, he had never exchanged confidences with
Kerrigan, much less listened to him justify his actions or behavior
for any reason, and as such he began to feel quite uncomfortable.
He tried to stop Kerrigan from saying any more, claiming that he
was not the person whose forgiveness Kerrigan needed to solicit,
but the captain was unmoved and uninterested in Arledge's
protests, and insisted that he could not go on unless he confessed
to someone—and who outside of Arledge would listen to his
story? First, he implored Arledge to communicate his very unworthy apology to Miss Cook, Captain Seebohm, and the rest of the
passengers, and also to recount all that he was about to tell—in
private and only if he considered it appropriate—to Miss
Bonington and Mr. Hugh Bayham, two people he felt might be

intelligent enough to understand all the things that had come to pass. Arledge, who had never seen Kerrigan so contrite and humble, felt even more awkward than before and tried to dissuade Kerrigan yet again, but his efforts were all in vain and his arguments completely ineffectual, either ignored or refuted by Kerrigan. And so the captain, more determined than ever, launched into a long and rather embarrassing monologue; more than a few people would have happily paid money not to hear it.

By the time Victor Arledge left Kerrigan's cabin an hour later, the expression on his face was a mixture of joy, fatigue, and stupor, and he walked about the upper deck very slowly, lost in thought, until finally he reached the lounge chairs by the stern and sat down. After a few moments, he got up, walked over to the railing, and rested his back against it, scanning the area just like a wizened old sailor, his eyes searching for the figures of Meffre and Bayham, who were nowhere to be seen. Finally, he flopped down on one of the green canvas lounge chairs, closed his eyes, and remained in this position for thirty-five minutes, during which time he pondered the subject of Kerrigan.

As the days went by, Arledge's need—perhaps an infelicitous word, but appropriate nonetheless—to learn the true story of Bayham's kidnapping only grew more acute. He soon concluded that it was time to abandon his "delicate" approach and address Bayham directly, but he couldn't seem to find the right moment to do so, which only exasperated him more. Just like the other passengers—though for different reasons—he had long since forgotten what on earth he was doing on the boat, and his long, lonely strolls on the upper deck were his principal activity now that there were no more port calls—the travelers had surrendered to the whims of the scientific researchers on that point—or conversations to distract his thoughts. Though he had never seriously considered the possibility that Bayham's adventures had ended at the moment when, according to Handl, the pianist had said they had, Arledge was by now so obsessed that, had he even briefly toyed with this notion now, he would have found it equally or even more unacceptable. Blinded by this fixation, he began to look at Bayham as a hateful man who derived pleasure from torturing him with his obstinate silence.

Of all the passengers, Hugh Everett Bayham reacted the most positively to Kerrigan's arrest. Always discreet, never overbearing, he did everything he could to raise his companions' spirits, most especially those of Florence Bonington and her father, who had been very affected by the incident. He spent hours on end in the lounges, doing his best to entertain everyone with jokes, quips, and charades, reading aloud the most pertinent news and compelling articles from the newspapers, and he even went so far as to organize a masquerade ball that was unfortunately foiled by the boat's excessive rocking to and fro on the evening in question. In addition to all this, as if to demonstrate his great generosity of character, he even asked after Captain Kerrigan's health on one or two occasions.

It was always either at twilight, after the Boningtons had retired for the evening, or very early in the morning, as he waited for them to emerge from their cabins, when Bayham would head for the lounge chairs on the upper deck and spend some time playing solitaire in the silent company of Victor Arledge and Léonide Meffre. These were the only moments that Arledge had any opportunity to speak with him, because at all other hours of the day the pianist was far too busy devoting his attentions to the Bonington family, and his efforts had paid off: Bayham had insinuated himself quite well into the father-and-daughter coterie, and the three of them created an inseparable, exclusive, and oddly impersonal group that, aside from being rather unapproachable, was also somehow rather unappealing. Perhaps Victor Arledge should have realized, during those monotonous days, that Hugh Everett Bayham's personality—still slightly a mystery to him at that

point—was probably neither strong nor very magnetic, and Arledge might have ventured to conclude that the reasons for his
mysterious trip to Scotland, whatever they were, deserved neither
such attention, such loss of sleep, nor, later on, the utter desolation
that stayed with him until his death. For the duration of that voyage, however, the perspicacity for which Victor Arledge was renowned all but abandoned him and, blinded by a simple curiosity
that had become something dangerously close to fanaticism, he
was unable to separate people's virtues from their shortcomings. It
was in this state of mind that he began to regard Léonide Meffre,
the one person who stood in the way of all his plans, with a hatred
that was truly excessive. The French poet, who adored the feeling
of the light breeze that wafted over the *Tallahassee*'s stern, spent
most of the day stretched out on a lounge chair at this end of the
boat, and as such his presence, albeit unwittingly, was the obstacle
that kept Arledge from achieving his objective. He never retired
before Bayham did in the evening, and always arrived before him
in the morning. Arledge, never losing hope that one day this pattern might be broken, would get up at dawn and, forgoing breakfast, would walk to the appointed spot at the stern and pray to the
heavens above that Bayham had arisen earlier than usual and that
Meffre had died during the night.

The days went by and the men slowly grew accustomed to
seeing one another on deck and slowly the conversation between
them became more frequent and more interesting, as well.
Whereas before they had limited their interchanges to the briefest
of greetings, they now chatted about things like the news, which
would often give way to longer exchanges—usually about some
trivial, inane topic—that, on certain occasions, actually caused
Bayham to arrive late to his appointments with the Boningtons.
Arledge, who considered Meffre a dismal conversationalist, was
convinced that this progress was due exclusively to the very high
opinion Bayham had formed of him the day that they had both

disagreed with the French poet during their conversation about the kidnapper Raisuli. All this, as such, led him to assume that Bayham might be well disposed to respond to his questions, and this conviction was what drove Victor Arledge to commit an act that, given his cold temperament, was certainly not the main reason that drove him to seek refuge in a distant relative's country home and abandon his writing career, but undoubtedly played a role in making Victor Arledge's last few years on earth a living nightmare.

Victor Arledge knew full well that Léonide Meffre was a proud, obstinate man, and for this reason what he did could not possibly have been an accident but rather, quite probably, an intentional act that was meticulously planned down to the very last detail. In mapping out his strategy, he had all but discarded the idea of recounting Kerrigan's story to Bayham and Miss Bonington mainly because the idea had seemed impractical and quite possibly mad, especially since Kerrigan had suggested it in an altered state of mind that seemed to have robbed him of his rational judgment. However, once Arledge finally decided how to set the scene that would give him the opportunity to question Bayham about his adventure, Kerrigan's bizarre request suddenly became useful to him and he decided to honor it, even though he knew full well that Kerrigan had had a change of heart—thanks to one of Fordington-Lewthwaite's thugs, who had told him so—and no longer wanted Arledge to tell them the story.

One morning, on the upper deck with Bayham and Meffre, Arledge began talking about piano recitals, and stated that most contemporary pianists, in general, were terrible when it came to Schubert's waltzes, playing them as if they were frivolous, trivial pieces unworthy of their virtuosity. Bayham, in part because he took it personally, in part because he was genuinely interested in the topic, enthusiastically began talking while Meffre sat back, more of a spectator in this conversation, and the minutes raced by as Bayham and Arledge debated away. Bayham was truly delighted by the topic (Brahms and Schumann, his favorite composers), and as such completely forgot about his appointment with the Boningtons. This had happened before on occasion, though never to this extent: after forty-five minutes of animated conversation, Florence Bonington suddenly appeared, dressed in yellow and carrying a parasol, and laughingly dismissed Bayham's hasty apologies. With a smile that softened her severe words, she proceeded to chide him for his negligence and for the lack of interest that his lateness so clearly revealed. Meffre soon joined this impromptu comedic scene with titters and comments that were somewhat out of place, and after a few minutes, when the joke had died down, Bayham offered Miss Bonington his arm and bid farewell to the two gentlemen. That was when Arledge, feigning surprise, exclaimed: "Oh no! Don't tell me you're leaving us! I was particularly glad that you came by just now, Miss Bonington, because I have been waiting for some time now to find the two of you together. I have something I must tell you with regard to Captain Kerrigan, something very confidential. First of all, he asked me to apologize to you, and then he asked me to tell you about a few things that might help you understand and, hopefully, forgive his behavior. I would be so grateful if you would be willing to take a few minutes to hear me out."

The young couple seemed to vacillate for a few moments until finally the pianist, after peering into young Miss Bonington's eyes and receiving the appropriately affirmative response, replied: "As you wish, Mr. Arledge, as long as it doesn't take too much of our time."

"No more than half an hour."

"Fine, then," said Florence. "But if you please, I'd like to tell my father that we are here with you."

With a light, graceful step, Miss Bonington disappeared. The three men were alone again, and for a few seconds silence reigned supreme. They looked at each other and then Arledge turned to Meffre and said: "I believe I mentioned before that the story I have been asked to tell Mr. Bayham and Miss Bonington is confidential. It is of an exceedingly delicate nature and involves a very private matter that I am only authorized to tell two people in particular. To do otherwise would be inappropriate and an abuse of trust on my part. Mr. Meffre, I sincerely regret having to ask this of you, and I beg your pardon for it, but I must ask you to kindly leave us alone for no more than thirty minutes."

Léonide Meffre sat up in his lounge chair, looked squarely in Arledge's eyes, and said, "Do you mean to say that you want me to leave?"

"Yes, if you would be so kind; if you are a gentleman."

"Are you suggesting I am something other than a gentleman?"

"Not at all; I know you are and for that reason I expect you will honor my request."

"And what if I decided not to?"

"I would be disappointed with you. Is that, then, your intention?"

"I haven't decided," replied Meffre, insolently leaning back down in his lounge chair.

"Mr. Meffre, I hardly think it so extraordinary to ask that you leave us alone for a short while. I assure you that I would not do so if I could think of another place on this boat where we might be as undisturbed as we are here. You know as well as I do that there is no other place for us to sit and talk; the cabins are far too small and moreover are devilishly hot at this hour of the day."

Meffre sat up again and, quite straightforwardly, asked this impertinent question: "Did it ever occur to you that I might be interested in Captain Kerrigan's secret life? And not just that: did it ever occur to you that I might be as offended as anyone else by his behavior, and feel that an explanation is owed me as well?"

"Your first question, Mr. Meffre, only deserves the deepest

scorn, and as for the second, Captain Kerrigan asked me to apologize to all the passengers on his behalf. I believe I already did that, in front of you, I might add, and as such I do not believe you are owed any more than that. The story I have been entrusted to tell Mr. Bayham and Miss Bonington is something of an entirely different nature and, as I said before, I do not have permission to tell it to anyone else."

"Captain Kerrigan doesn't have to know."

"Mr. Meffre, your words offend me deeply. Do you believe me to have no sense of responsibility whatsoever?"

At this point, Bayham decided to intervene: "In light of Mr. Meffre's attitude, perhaps we would be wise to leave this for some other time, Mr. Arledge."

"It's too late for that, Mr. Bayham. Mr. Meffre has gone too far with his audacity and boorish manners. We cannot simply get up and leave now. For the last time, Mr. Meffre, are you going to leave us alone or not? We are wasting a great deal of time here and Mr. Bonington is waiting for his daughter and Mr. Bayham."

At that very moment Florence reappeared, having caught the tail end of Arledge's comment. Flustered, the young woman timidly asked what was going on. Nobody said a word until Meffre sarcastically replied, "Mr. Arledge: nobody but Fordington-Lewthwaite can force me to leave this spot. Why don't you speak with him about it?" With a flourish, he grabbed one of his newspapers, opened it, and began to read.

"Mr. Meffre, I warn you for the last time: either comply with the favor I have very courteously asked of you, or I will be obliged to teach you a lesson."

Meffre put the newspaper down and spun around to face Arledge, furious.

"Are you threatening me?"

"Yes, I am. I couldn't have said it better myself."

Florence, who by now had picked up on what was happening,

tried to diffuse the tension.

"Gentlemen, please be reasonable. This is hardly worth such a fuss."

"Perhaps not before, Miss Bonington," said Arledge. "But now it has become a personal matter between myself and Mr. Meffre— between myself and this insolent imbecile."

The insult had finally bubbled up and spilled from Arledge's lips, and Meffre reacted as one might have expected. He jumped to his feet at once, stormed over to the novelist, and punched him squarely in the jaw.

"I suffer insults from nobody, Mr. Arledge. I demand immediate satisfaction."

Arledge could not hide the slight but very triumphant smile that came over his face, and said: "As you wish, Mr. Meffre. Tomorrow at dawn, then. Mr. Bayham and Mr. Tourneur will be my seconds, if they have no objection."

"Arledge, think about what you are doing," said the pianist. "Please, think it over carefully."

"Are you willing to be my second?"

"Yes, of course," Bayham dutifully replied.

"We ought to decide on the weapon," said Meffre.

"Pistols."

"Fine. I will be waiting for you here at six in the morning. I trust you won't miss the date."

"You can be certain of that, sir. I'll let you take care of supplying the weapons—if it isn't an inconvenience, that is, and if you can find them."

"I'll get them, don't worry about that."

Meffre turned away, leaned back in his lounge chair, opened his newspaper again, and quickly busied himself reading. Arledge turned to Bayham and Florence, smiled, and said: "I am so sorry you had to witness such a sordid incident. As if that weren't enough, I've wasted your valuable time, and I cannot forgive myself for that. Please do offer my apologies to your father, Miss Bonington, for having kept you here so pointlessly. I am afraid Kerrigan's story is just going to have to wait until tomorrow."

Bayham and Florence, visibly affected by the scene they had just witnessed, murmured a few words of encouragement, or perhaps courtesy, and disappeared from sight. Victor Arledge then settled down in the lounge chair next to Léonide Meffre, lit a cigarette, and gazed out at the crisscrossing whitecaps the *Tallahassee* left behind in its wake.

Fordington-Lewthwaite reacted to the latest turn of events in the most predictable fashion: highly conscious of his responsibilities as potential future captain of the *Tallahassee,* he flew into a rage at first, mostly because he was infuriated that a duel had been held on board without his knowledge. But after a short while, especially given that his sense of honor was sketchy at best, he eventually accepted the news with total serenity and, fearful of the complaints that the travelers might register with his superiors once the trip came to an end if he allowed his capricious feelings to get the best of him, he proceeded, unceremoniously and almost surreptitiously, as if he didn't want the other passengers to see, to throw the body of Léonide Meffre overboard.

The death of the French poet did not come as a surprise to those who were close to Arledge and, as such, knew of his proficiency with firearms. The English novelist had proven this on three other occasions, while Mr. Meffre—who, until then, had always managed to wiggle his way out of the challenges that his incorrigible impertinence frequently provoked—was a complete novice in such matters. Because of this, the reason behind his very imprudent impulse to challenge Victor Arledge remains a minor mystery. Whether he was emboldened by his hatred for the writer, his desire to impress Miss Bonington (there was no concrete proof that he adored her, but there was none to the contrary, either), or simply because he had lost control of his emotions, we may never know. And had Léonide Meffre been a truly first-rate author, perhaps his story would now occupy the time and thoughts of some innocent and diligent biographer. But alas, that is not the case.

There was little to say about the duel: Arledge, having been the offended party, had the right to take the first shot, which was, in the end, the only shot. The bullet lodged itself firmly in the forehead of Mr. Meffre, who crumpled without even a whimper, and most certainly without sufficient time to realize that he had been wounded. His seconds, the horrified Mr. Littlefield and Mr. Beauvais, somber and quite devastated, picked his body up off the floor and, without a word, carried it away. The dry shot, luckily, had not awakened any of the other passengers, and even the sailors on lookout had just fallen asleep as dawn broke. Lederer Tourneur, distressed but convinced that justice had been served, followed them for about a minute, as Arledge and Bayham, indifferent but perhaps slightly upset, walked in the direction of Fordington-Lewthwaite's cabin with the intention of informing him of what had just transpired.

Léonide Meffre was not a pleasant person, as everyone knew, nor was he interesting in any sense. Nevertheless, the other passengers did not share the animosity and scorn Arledge felt for him; they simply saw him as a mediocre man who fancied himself a distinguished gentleman and an important poet. They knew him to be boring, vulgar, uninspired, loquacious, indiscreet, and frequently annoying but, for all intents and purposes, totally harmless. For this reason, his death did not make much of an impression upon the passengers of the *Tallahassee,* who were so fatigued that they could no longer experience any more shock or pain as they normally had before and, rather indifferently, they decided to adopt the easiest and most logical attitude of all, which was that of simply not addressing—though not forgetting—the event that had come to pass. Perhaps it would be unfair to call Miss Bonington an innocent for expecting Arledge to feel, if not regret, then at least some measure of chagrin for the death of his adversary, because for the record, she had no idea of what kind of man Arledge really was, nor was she at all aware of the elaborate ruses and premeditated calculations with which Arledge had orchestrated his every move onboard the *Tallahassee*. Innocent or not, however, this was what Miss Bonington expected of Arledge—at first with confidence and as time went by with growing indignation, and always in vain. Had it not been for this minor detail, the death of Léonide Meffre would have been entirely inconsequential, serving no other purpose than that which Arledge had originally intended. But now that certain unexpected emotions had suddenly entered the fray— emotions that Arledge had not anticipated and that, due to his inexperience, made him vulnerable and helpless—it seemed that, yet again, his plans might be doomed to fail and his objectives delayed indefinitely. The indifference with which the other travelers digested the news of the duel and its result did little to mollify Miss Bonington—if anything, in fact, it made her angrier. Had the displeasure been collective and the continued existence of Victor Arledge unanimously condemned, the young woman's violent reaction would have gone unnoticed, and her accusations would have been superfluous, but, unseconded and delivered with an almost adolescent fury, they had dismal consequences for the novelist's pretensions. Miss Bonington, whose terrible distress following Meffre's death may have stemmed from her guilt at not having done anything to prevent it when she could have, first rebuked Hugh Everett Bayham for having participated in an act she considered tantamount to murder. The pianist, instead of defending the parameters of the duel—as he had done before—simply justified his presence on deck at six in the morning by claiming that, as a gentleman, there was no way he could refuse a friend who requested his support in such circumstances, especially when the friend asked for it as directly as Arledge had. It would be inter-

esting indeed to find out the exact terms of the relationship between Bayham and Miss Bonington—and I am afraid that Victor
Arledge did—but from what I have been able to ascertain to date,
I imagine it was the type of relationship—the observation of
which, I admit, is rather agonizing and often leads to the de-
humanization of one of the two parties—that often arises between
young couples on the precipice of getting married. This type of
relationship usually exhibits two distinct characteristics: the most
absolute servility (or dutiful resignation) on the side of the truly
enamored party (in this case Hugh Everett Bayham), and the fickle
whim of the other (in this case Florence Bonington) who, conscious of his or her charms, and as such doubly pernicious, simply
allows him or herself to be admired and loved. In the majority of
cases, and contrary to what one might intuitively guess, this second party is usually the less intelligent of the two. I realize this may
be a simplistic and slightly rudimentary way to look at it, but it
does seem to explain, quite perfectly, the reasons why Hugh
Everett Bayham, the day after Léonide Meffre's death, decided he
would not set foot on the upper deck. As I suggested, the pianist
made this decision under terrible duress, and it is entirely likely
that the word *reasoning* cannot fairly be applied in this instance.
Perhaps the motivation at work was instinct and an awkward
process of idea-association, compounded by his beloved's antipa-
thy for the English novelist, who had only been partially responsible for setting the chain of events in motion but, unfortunately,
would be forced to suffer all its worst consequences.

When a person is concentrated on achieving a specific goal,
there is always a moment at which either the path toward achieving that goal becomes terribly arduous and difficult, or else, if the
interests are lasting ones, progress (or lack thereof) is gradual: this,
then, is the point at which the person in question suddenly comes
up with what might be termed a "transcendental alternative." It is
very possible that, as the boat sailed from Alexandria, this was pre-

cisely the kind of alternative Victor Arledge suddenly believed had materialized before him, and right then made a decision that, later on, he would postpone in favor of the exact opposite decision, inspired by what he foolishly considered such a significant step forward in his relationship with Hugh Everett Bayham that he had no qualms about suddenly throwing all caution to the wind. But this very clearly indicated that his interests hadn't quite mellowed to the point that he actually needed to avail himself of the afore-mentioned transcendental alternative, and for that reason—for having already enjoyed the privilege of deciding on another occasion, that is, for already having gone through that experience—when the real need truly arrived, you might say that it caught him by surprise, and he felt confused, bewildered, and hesitant. By that point, Victor Arledge had already found himself, on two separate occasions, obliged to conquer prejudice, ignore misgivings, and act according to the dictates of his imagination, ignoring the rules and principles that had made him the conservative, lucid man he was. And each of these occasions or decisions was followed by the most absolute certainty that, once his plans had been executed, he would be able to carry out his ultimate objectives. But his objectives, which at first consisted of nothing more than finding out exactly what had happened to Hugh Everett Bayham in Scotland and why, had changed over time. His objective—that is, the thing he most wanted but couldn't achieve, the thing that constituted his lasting commitment to the more arduous and difficult path—had changed after the violent death of Léonide Meffre. His primary interest now was that of drawing Hugh Everett Bayham into a conversation and maintaining it. In truth, all his obsession, obstinacy, and obfuscation stemmed from the fact that Bayham had refused to satisfy his curiosity, rather than from his earlier desires, which had been driven by idle interest. For all these reasons, Miss Bonington's attitude following the latest turn of events, as well as the reasons behind her fierce reproach, were a terrible blow for

Arledge, the impact of which he did not even try to attenuate with the kind of unfounded optimism that usually drives people never to give up. He would have to react with patience to this new setback, and that was when he really had to make a decision regarding the dilemma now facing him: luck was not on his side, and despite his many sly stratagems, he had not managed to achieve his objectives. Coming back to the real world for a few moments, he gazed out at the coastline and identified the direction in which the *Tallahassee* was headed. At nightfall, as he rested his elbows against the rail and looked out onto the Algerian coast, he actually asked himself if all his painstaking troubles were worth the effort. A whole barrage of images, places, and events that he had long since forgotten suddenly paraded through his mind: his apartment on the Rue Buffault, the Theatre Antoine, Mme D'Almeida, Kerrigan's visit to his home, Handl's letter, his sister's apartment, the recent death of his friend Francis Linnell, the train trip he had been obliged to take in order to say goodbye to his parents, Colonel McLiam, the port at Marseilles, and a few verses by Jones Very. He then lit a cigarette, and without realizing it, let the match burn all the way down to his fingers. Suddenly he threw the match into the water and rubbed his hand against his elegant, beige-colored jacket. Then, as if deeply fatigued, he breathed in the twilight breeze and, leaning against the cane with the gold-and-marble hilt that he occasionally carried with him—most of the time just as a decorative touch—he walked toward the stultifying heat of his cabin.

BOOK FIVE

"**T**he adventures of Captain Kerrigan could hardly be summed up in a single conversation, and for this reason I truly apologize for lacking the precision that some of my colleagues most certainly possess, but I will try, insofar as I am able, to faithfully render what he told me, and I will also do my best not to forget (that is, omit), from such a massive accumulation of facts and picturesque scenarios, the basic purpose of his story, and at the same time I will try to be as rigorously detailed as time allows.

"As you may already know, Kerrigan spent the greater part of his life traveling from one place to another: we can safely say that up until five years ago—that is, September '99—which is when he settled into a comfortable apartment in Paris, he never remained in the same place for more than two or three months at a time—with the exception of, precisely, the period about which I am about to describe to you. His story began in 1863, when he was fourteen years old and left his home in Raleigh. But wait, please wait: I don't think I am telling this story very well. I fear that with this lengthy introduction—somewhat incoherent, precisely because it is not premeditated in any way—I am only delaying the essential element of this tale and boring you, neither of which I wish to do. There is no reason, of course, that you should find the story amusing or pleasant. It is neither amusing nor pleasant, but at least in theory and principle, it should never be boring. Perhaps you noticed the date I mentioned, the date Kerrigan left his family home, never to return: 1863. In effect, he did this so that he could join the army despite his very tender age and, as I was able to glean during one of our exhausting sessions together, he fought tirelessly all the way through to the end of the war. When he returned home, he found his home in ruins, burned and sacked. The bodies of his father, mother, and sister were nowhere to be found, though he did not spend any time searching for them, as did many other soldiers, for the likelihood of finding them was, in those days and under those circumstances, minimal at best. The families that had managed to survive the Sherman and Schofield marches had sought refuge in the most astonishing places and, on occasion, when they were able, many of them began the long journey out west and never looked back. In addition, Kerrigan knew that his brother Alastair had perished in the most wretched manner imaginable during the second battle of Bull Run. From that very moment—well, in actuality, long before that, when he had first left his house for the front—Kerrigan decided that the one and only way he would survive in this world was if he never wasted time worrying about himself, and with that in mind he decided to blaze his own path, the only clear and definite goal of which, from that day forward, was to become a very wealthy man. I myself have never had to brandish a firearm on the fields of battle, but I imagine that such an experience calls for a very complex kind of determination that requires a man to abandon every last scruple he may possess. This, then, was what Kerrigan became when he was sixteen or seventeen years old: a man without scruples. Now, this is not to imply that Kerrigan tried to justify all

the crimes he committed by invoking his introduction to war at
such a young age, but I do believe he wanted me to see that, given
his circumstances in 1865, after having been defeated, and with
only the vaguest understanding of French and gentlemanly
knowledge, his only choice in life was to become, categorically
and unrepentantly, a hard and even cruel man. It would be impossible to count the number of crimes and misdeeds Kerrigan has
committed in the course of his audacious, intrepid existence, and
I will not be the one to divulge them, for two basic reasons: first,
Kerrigan and I have come to be friends—perhaps not in the con-
ventional sense of the word, but nonetheless it would be neither
elegant nor appropriate of me to reveal—even with his consent—
the details regarding his excesses which, moreover, he fully and
wholeheartedly regrets. The second reason is simpler and perhaps
less noble: nobody would want to listen to the litany of his bloody
exploits, which range from robbery to dismemberment, rape, slave
trafficking, betrayal, murder, torture, criminal fraud, embezzle-
ment, defamation, libel, and calumny. Please do forgive me, but
I feel incapable of repeating, word for word, all the things Kerrigan
confessed to me just a few days ago. After all, the thing that concerns us, the thing that, to some degree or other, drove him to lock
himself up with five bottles of whisky and later on commit such
condemnable acts on the upper deck of the boat, endangering the
life of, among others, Miss Bonington, who is your... fiancée, is
that right? Please, don't bother answering that, it makes no difference whatsoever, it is simply, once again, my very reprehensible,
insatiable, and unquenchable desire to know everything and has
very little to do with the lost soul of whom I just spoke. I will tell
you, however, because I want to stop you from forming the opinion that I know is now taking root in your head—I can tell by the
incredulous look in your eyes—that the Captain Kerrigan you see
today is not a despicable, miserable, perverse, or contemptible
person. The change that has taken place inside of him over the

course of so many years is quite remarkable, and as such, we find ourselves today facing a very typical case of a man tormented by his past, filled with regret for almost everything he did, but who has at last found some measure of redemption. For this reason, I beg of you, please do not judge him too severely; bear in mind that it was Kerrigan himself who asked me to tell you this story in the hope that you, Mr. Bayham, and Miss Bonington (whose absence, I must admit, is a relief) might be able to understand him, if not forgive him. It is terribly important to him, and I feel it is to his credit.

"The year was 1892, and Kerrigan, a prematurely aging, bankrupt man of forty-three, was living in the port city of Amoy, on the Straits of Formosa. He had been living in the East and South China Seas for seven long years, during which time he devoted himself to the trafficking of all types of merchandise—legitimately on occasion, but more often than not, via illegal methods. He was not, however, a large-scale contraband trafficker; what I mean is that his rather smallish boats did not make very long-distance runs. The products he transported were never from Europe or America, and his business was generally limited to the South China and Java Seas, the Bay of Bengal, and, on extremely exceptional occasions—to carry out, for example, the transfer of highly valued goods or a particular shipment whose illegal transport was punished especially severely—the Gulf of Oman. You could say, then, that he was a small-time local smuggler; I realize that the distances I mention are certainly considerable, but that is, nonetheless, the term used for traffickers who operate within those coordinates. And while Hong Kong, Macau, Shanghai, Singapore, and Batavia were the real hubs of trade in this part of the world, Kerrigan's ambitions were relatively modest, and so he set up shop in Amoy, gambling on the assumption that the competition would be negligible given that it was a second- or third-rate port at best, with poor police protection, and more opportunities to find good offers for mediocre products, which was generally what was available in that country. His business, as you may imagine, was neither impressive nor profitable, but seven years is a long time and, slowly but surely, Kerrigan became a very wealthy man. With the aid of a business partner, he founded a shipping company some two years before he finally went bankrupt, and though it was a relatively insignificant outfit—he had only about a dozen vessels making runs between Amoy and Malaca, Singapore and Bintalu, Fu-Cheu and Luzón—the company began to show earnings in a very short period of time. As such, Kerrigan and his partner, a German by the name of Lutz, began to enjoy an embarrassment of riches and became the local kingpins of Amoy. With plenty of money in their coffers, they became moneylenders and, with the impunity afforded them by their status as Westerners, began exploiting the natives. The interest rates they charged the trusting local population were exorbitant, and whenever someone was unable to pay what they owed Kerrigan within the agreed-upon periods and terms, Lutz, a rubicund man with a harsh complexion who was capable of even greater cruelty than Kerrigan, hunted them down and ruthlessly beat them until they died. Lutz, you see, was a truly fearsome, insolent, despotic man. Not just corpulent but fat, with a red face that was crowned by a strawlike mat of curly blond hair, he was just short of forty years old. Everything about him was a rosy pink, and whenever he got excited or angry his face would swell up in the most alarming way and a thick vein would appear on his forehead or neck, depending on the season of the year. He always wore the same clothes: a wrinkled white suit with pants that were always a bit too wide, a pair of short black boots that were a real eyesore (perhaps because they contrasted so sharply with his generally bedraggled look), light blue or beige shirts, and a garnet-colored tie so wide that it completely covered his voluminous belly when he opened the buttons on his vest. To this outfit he occasionally added a worn-out Panama hat and an eccentric cane.

His eyes were tiny and their color indecipherable, his chin nonexistent and his nose unquestionably German. Of average height, he seemed short and out of proportion due to the excess fat on his body, and though he cinched his belt very high above his waist, his legs inevitably seemed extremely short. In the mornings he usually took a stroll down by the port to oversee his team of workers, and though the natives snickered at him behind his back, his presence in any part of the city inspired fear and respect. Kerrigan was every bit as ruthless as Lutz, to be sure, but his goals were far more abstract and ambitious, and for this reason he allowed the German to occupy himself with the more public affairs of the business, so to speak: dealing with subordinates, collecting payments, bribing the authorities, and acting as the visible head of the Kerrigan & Lutz Shipping and Lending Company, while Kerrigan focused on the company's internal administration. For this reason Lutz was the man who always struck fear in the hearts of the city's residents and listened to all their petitions and requests. Accustomed to dealing with him and suffering his frequent explosions of rage, the people of Amoy considered Lutz their master and the owner of the company, when in reality Lutz was often just carrying out orders that Kerrigan very wisely dispensed in the form of suggestions. Needless to say, Kerrigan was the real brain and force behind Kerrigan & Lutz, not only because he was far more intelligent and astute but because our captain, before settling down in Amoy, had held countless different jobs, more than a few of which were quite similar to his undertakings in the Chinese port city. Lutz's contribution to the business, on the other hand, was primarily financial. He and Kerrigan had met in Africa ten years earlier, a time when both men's professional endeavors revolved around the slave trade. Kerrigan, perhaps having decided that the business was simply too despicable (as I believe I mentioned, his misgivings came slowly and grudgingly), abandoned it rather abruptly, but Lutz stayed on for four more years, eventually becoming a tremendously wealthy man. With all the money he amassed, he soon found himself forced to flee the African continent as the laws of various African countries began to catch up with him, and he ended up in Batavia with no particular plan for the future. There, he began to chip away at the fortune he had accumulated—primarily in the Sudan—until the day that Kerrigan, on a routine visit to the city, ran into him and suggested they go into business together. Lutz was a dim, rather short-sighted, coarse man who lived according to no plan and spent money as quickly as he earned it. For him, there was no future other than the most immediate, and while he readily agreed to participate in Kerrigan's enterprise, he did so only because when Kerrigan suggested it he had nothing better to do, no interesting exploits on the horizon, and not because, like Kerrigan, he figured he was getting close to retiring, and had decided that settling down in some specific place with some specific business was the best way to slow down and plan for a more stable future. That was really the moment, you see, when Captain Kerrigan started to seriously consider putting an end to all his constant traveling—after all, it was only seven years before he finally settled down in Paris. Eager to keep his partner happy, Kerrigan basically let Lutz do more or less what he wanted, which, in addition, kept him away from certain matters, such as bookkeeping and business contracts, that did not concern him. I don't mean to say that Kerrigan was cheating his partner; knowing Lutz the way he did, I sincerely doubt that ever crossed his mind. And Lutz, though not intelligent, was most definitely a crafty fellow—not for nothing had he operated on the fringes of the law all his life without ever getting caught or punished for it, and he made a point of reviewing Kerrigan's books once a month, checking the numbers with painstaking attention to detail. Even though he was a partner in the business, he preferred to take in a weekly salary from Kerrigan rather than deal with all the balance sheets, budgets, expense deductions, and other tables and charts necessary to calculate the

amounts he was due from their net earnings. As such, he allowed—
and I would even say thanked—Kerrigan to take care of this aspect
of things while he simply made sure to review the American
gentleman's work to ensure that he wasn't being swindled. Lutz,
most definitely, was interested in other, more despicable activities.
But the method he worked out for earning his money was not
perfect and, in fact, had one grave flaw: the sums Lutz received
every week were, obviously, somewhat reduced. And so, just as he
had always done at all the other times in his turbulent life when
he had any money, Lutz spent it as fast as he earned it. And while
Kerrigan, who removed from the cash box the precise amount of
money he had coming to him every month, either saved or in-
vested almost all of his personal earnings, Lutz sometimes actually
found himself forced to ask Kerrigan to disburse his weekly pay-
ment twenty-four or sometimes forty-eight hours in advance, such
was the velocity at which he consumed his salary. And this
occurred primarily because Lutz was simply incapable of manag-
ing his affairs. Kerrigan had made his home out of three empty
rooms in the building, a one-story wooden affair that housed
Kerrigan & Lutz, while Lutz lived in the city's only European
hotel. Kerrigan lived more than comfortably but without luxuries,
while Lutz squandered his money as if he hadn't a care in the
world. Kerrigan lived a rather austere existence, while Lutz's could
only be described as reckless. For all these reasons, not to mention
the countless hours he whiled away in the city's many opium dens,
at this point Lutz was far poorer than he had been when he had
arrived at Amoy, and while he may not have realized this during
the first six months of his partnership with Kerrigan, he did begin
to take notice soon thereafter, and it became difficult to ignore
when, after a year in business together, Kerrigan offered to buy out
Lutz's share. It happened at Kerrigan's house, during a dinner in
honor of Kerrigan & Lutz's first anniversary. The festivities were
in full swing; it was an evening of sparkle and good cheer, and they

were just starting to sample their desserts when Lutz—who, contrary to what one would guess, never drank at all—decided to
make an exception to his rule so that he could toast to the continued success and prosperity of 'the firm,' as he called it. Kerrigan,
as we know, is not at all abstemious, and that night he had drunk
far more than his fair share of alcohol. Believing Lutz's toast to be
sarcastic, Kerrigan mistakenly thought that his intentions had been
revealed; awkward, flustered, and totally unprepared, not having
had the chance to prepare his speech or figure out how to break
it to Lutz, he made his offer in front of all the other guests. Lutz,
unable to hide his shock, remained frozen in his chair. But
Kerrigan, drunk as he was, kept on talking, trying to come up with
arguments that might justify his acquisition attempt and at the
same time preserve the dignity of the crestfallen German who, for
once in his life more astute than his partner, simply kept his mouth
shut and allowed Kerrigan to reveal his ideas. When Kerrigan was
finished, Lutz raised his glass high, repeated his toast, and downed
the contents in one long gulp. When he was done, Kerrigan made
his own toast and waited to see what Lutz would say or do. Lutz
then stood up, gathered his hat and cane, walked to the door,
turned to Kerrigan to bid him farewell, and said: 'I will think about
it.' With that, he was gone.

"Some time passed before either man dared mention the anniversary dinner and what had transpired that night. Given that
Lutz had said he would think about it, Kerrigan did not want to
press the issue for fear that his partner would fly into a rage—he
was, of course, perfectly willing to confront Lutz and kill him if
necessary, but he preferred to avoid that if possible—and decided
to give him all the time he needed to make his decision. Lutz, for
his part, continued inspecting the docks and roughing up the local
population as he always did, as if nothing at all had changed. One
month went by in this fashion, and Kerrigan began to suspect that
Lutz was orchestrating something, even though his behavior, on

the surface, did not suggest this in the least. To this end, Kerrigan decided to take action and began to send Lutz on business trips. Alleging that the employees of the vessels handling their smuggled goods were making unplanned stops at Hong Kong and Victoria and selling part of their shipments without their consent, pocketing the profits of such sales which, naturally, they did not declare, Kerrigan suggested that it would be very useful for one of them—none of their employees could be trusted with such a task—to personally escort the cargo and take a more active role in its transfer and delivery. Now, there was no way Kerrigan could abandon his administrative duties; his presence was all but required in Amoy, whereas Lutz's duties could easily be relegated to a couple of thugs. Lutz, of course, was not particularly enthused by the idea of spending long periods of time outside Amoy, but there was no way to argue with Kerrigan, and he soon took charge of the company's trips to the Bay of Bengal and the Java Sea. Both Kerrigan and Lutz were experts in their chosen fields, and as such their expeditions were not terrifically dangerous for Lutz, who knew all the navigation routes by heart, especially those the authorities tended to overlook, and he was also quite adept at dodging pursuers, including the British police boats that constantly patrolled those waters. On many occasions, however, the cargo would arrive late at the cities—Madras and Singapore, in general—that provided them with their merchandise, and Lutz and his boats would be obliged to wait around for several weeks, which meant that the German's trips would stretch on, sometimes for more than two months at a time. It goes without saying, of course, that Lutz only made these trips when the merchandise was very delicate or valuable. But these trips left Kerrigan free to do whatever he wished in Amoy. First and foremost, he began to cheat Lutz out of a fair amount of money; always traveling, Lutz had no way of collecting his weekly salary, nor was he able to review the accounting books as frequently as he had before. Kerrigan now paid Lutz whenever he returned from one of his trips, but it was always less than what he was really owed. With this little ruse, Kerrigan had eliminated one of the risks he had envisioned: that Lutz had put off his response so that he might save money and get out of the very dire financial straits he had been in when Kerrigan had first proposed the buyout, and eventually achieve a certain level of financial stability. Kerrigan also took other measures: by distributing favors, he bought the loyalty of most of his employees and, right in his office, began to amass a veritable arsenal of weapons: shotguns, repeating rifles, munitions, gunpowder, pistols—insurance, so to speak, against whatever might happen if Lutz were to suddenly unleash his rage and attempt to take over the offices with a team of criminal thugs one day. All of this helped Kerrigan feel safer, and he now felt certain that the company would belong exclusively to him in a very short period of time. Lutz, what with all his comings and goings—the prosperous business they had created was in terribly high demand—had grown further and further away from the everyday administration of the firm and, in effect, had become a kind of foreman. To put it another way, his duties were no longer those of a wealthy co-owner, that much is for sure. The months went by and Lutz continued performing his duties, never once dropping even the slightest mention of the proposition Kerrigan had made on the night of the company's first anniversary. Kerrigan, at one point, actually began to wonder if perhaps Lutz had forgotten the episode entirely, and actually considered reiterating and raising his offer, even though the original one was quite lucrative indeed. Things went on like this until finally, eleven months after their anniversary celebration, Lutz exploded. As I mentioned before, on this latest spate of trips, the partner of the *Tallahassee*'s tormented captain generally went to Madras and Singapore, and Singapore was in fact where their shipments were most frequently delayed, a nuisance that forced Lutz to spend weeks and weeks waiting around with his boats docked in the harbor. This, it seems, allowed him to become familiar with, among other things, the city's customs and habits as well as its bars and taverns. About eleven months after that fateful night, as I mentioned, Lutz returned to Amoy following one of his trips to Singapore, but he did not arrive alone: he was accompanied by a tall, slender man with olive skin, some thirty-five years old, with blond hair, a thick moustache, and a rather baleful look in his eyes, which may have been due to an untreated case of myopia. The suit he wore was identical to Lutz's, just as wrinkled but better fitting; and he carried at least one massive pistol, the butt of which peeked out from the right-hand pocket of his trousers, hiking up the tail of his jacket and making it look even more wrinkled. From the window of his office at the Kerrigan & Lutz Shipping and Lending Company, Kerrigan watched the two men step off the boat and wondered who this new friend might be. He looked like a very determined fellow despite his rather lackluster appearance and the less-than-noble look in his eyes. In short, he looked like a rogue. The two men, instead of walking directly over to the company offices, turned down the road that led to the hotel where Lutz made his home, which made Kerrigan think that Lutz, in an uncharacteristic display of courtesy and good manners, had decided to escort his companion to his hotel and wait for him to take a bath and rest up from their journey before introducing him to Kerrigan and handing over the report of their recent undertaking in Singapore which had involved a shipment of extremely high-quality silk. Nevertheless, given the slightly unorthodox nature of the situation, Kerrigan took precautionary measures. First he sent a Chinese man over to the Hotel Cleveland to greet Lutz and his companion, and also to inquire after the results of the trip. Then he proceeded to load two of his pistols, placing the smaller of the two in one of his jacket pockets and the larger one in the main drawer of his desk. He also called two other employees and warned them to remain on their guard and to stay close to the building just in case he needed them. Once he was done with these preparations, he sat down in front of a window that looked out over both the commercial port and the hotel, and he sat there awaiting the arrival of Lutz and his friend with the confident stride and evasive gaze. The two subjects took their time, however, and it wasn't until a full hour and a half later that Kerrigan finally saw them leave the hotel and walk in the direction of the offices. During this period of time, the Chinese man Kerrigan had sent to the hotel returned, saying that Mr. Lutz had refused to receive him. Once he ascertained that Lutz and his new friend were most certainly walking toward the offices of Kerrigan & Lutz, Kerrigan moved away from the window, sat down, and scattered some papers and documents across his desk to make them believe that their arrival had in no way distracted him from his work. The distance between the hotel and the office building was considerable, and the captain had to peer out the window a few times to check up on how the two men were advancing. Both Lutz and his companion were now walking with a decisive stride, and Lutz was literally shining with glee, a sentiment that Kerrigan had not observed on his face since the now legendary evening, and this troubled him even more. Finally, back at his desk, Kerrigan could hear the sound of the two men's boots as they climbed the porch steps. This was followed by a light knock on the wooden door.

"'Come in,' he said. The door swung open, and the two men entered the building.

"Lutz, smiling from ear to ear, advanced toward Kerrigan and cordially offered him his outstretched hand, which Kerrigan shook. Lutz then turned to the tall, thin man, and introduced him as Mr. Kolldehoff, from Holland. Kerrigan stood up without moving away from the desk, shook Mr. Kolldehoff's hand, and, after inviting the two men to take a seat, sat back down in his own chair. Lutz and Kolldehoff quickly sat down, and Lutz began to speak. First he informed Kerrigan that the shipment had arrived, as usual, with no

problem, and added that he hoped Kerrigan would receive better
offers for the silk this time around, since the offer for their previous cargo had been somewhat disappointing. To this, Kerrigan
replied that he would do his best and then, turning to face
Kolldehoff, remarked that the competition was beginning to gain a
foothold in Amoy, and that it was no longer quite so easy to place
textiles at the prices they had been able to name five years earlier.
Kolldehoff simply nodded his head in silence. That was when
Kerrigan did something terribly imprudent, though I cannot imagine that the conversation would have turned out much differently
had he done otherwise. He turned to face Lutz and began to talk
about his next trip, this time to Batavia, to pick up a shipment of
cigars from America. He showered Lutz with all kinds of instructions and orders, underscoring how very important this merchandise was—after all, it was coming from the Americas—and then
told him he would have to make the run without his usual helms-
man, because Kerrigan had begun to doubt his loyalty. He proceeded to specify the route Lutz was to take, and then gave him the
password he would need to identify the man who would release
the boxes of cigars. As he did this, Kerrigan did not, for some reason, notice that Lutz's face grew darker and darker all the while.
Kolldehoff then turned to the German, flashed him an impatient
look, and Lutz slammed his fist down on the table. Kerrigan, surprised by the outburst, cut short his endless monologue as his left
hand instinctively gravitated to the desk drawer where he had
placed one of his pistols, and he opened the drawer ever so slightly as his right hand traveled to his jacket pocket. Lutz, with remarkable aplomb, stood up and declared that he could no longer delay
the very happy announcement he wished to make: at long last, he
was finally able to respond to the offer Kerrigan had made him
eleven months earlier. Our friend moved away from the desk just a
bit: 'And what is your response?'

"'I would like to buy you out, Kerrigan.'

"In all those months of waiting, this was the one scenario that Kerrigan had not foreseen, since he had never thought much of his partner's intelligence. Though he already knew the answer, he nevertheless pulled himself together, let out a cackle, and inquired sarcastically: 'With whose money, may I ask?'

"The German did not disappoint him: 'Mr. Kolldehoff's. He will be my new partner.'

"Kerrigan toyed with the idea of saying that he would think about it, just as Lutz had, but on one hand he doubted Lutz would be quite as gullible as he had been, and on the other hand he imagined that no matter what the two men would give him a deadline of some sort, anyway. For these reasons, he resolved to face his problem head-on and, removing the tiny pistol in his jacket pocket, pointed the gun at Lutz and Kolldehoff, and said: 'I'm sick of seeing your face around here, Lutz. I have been for a long time. I don't want to kill you or your friend, whom I've only just met and for whom I bear no ill will. You've been a dismal partner and you know better than anyone that this business belongs to me. It's the result of my ideas and my efforts. Now get out of here, both of you, and don't ever set foot in this building or I'll have no choice but to kill you. Have I made myself clear? If you leave me an address I'll send you your share of the money, although if you don't trust me to do that I wouldn't blame you. But it's your risk to take. Now get out. And I'm warning you, Lutz: I will kill you if you try anything. The same goes for you, Mr. Kolldehoff.'

"The two men walked backwards toward the door, opened it, and left. Before closing it, Lutz screamed out with fury: 'You'll be hearing from me, Kerrigan!'

"Kerrigan knew that Lutz wouldn't be scared off by a few simple threats, but he didn't kill him on the spot, as he himself confessed to me, because he was getting on in years and it was getting harder and harder for him to kill someone in cold blood. As he stood at the window and watched them walk away in the direction of the hotel, he knew that Lutz and Kolldehoff, the impassive Dutchman, would come back and try to murder him in a couple of days, once they had formulated a plan.

"Sure enough, three days went by, as calm and uneventful as could be imagined, and Kerrigan used this time to figure out the plan—or at least part of the plan—being hatched by his two adversaries. During those three days, Kerrigan's employees—whose loyalty, as you may recall, he had bought during Lutz's extended absences—began to disappear, slowly and seemingly mysteriously, and I say 'seemingly' because Kerrigan was absolutely certain that Kolldehoff and his money were bribing the men to abandon him. But Kerrigan understood the Chinese, and moreover he understood their peculiar concept of friendship: he had bought them not with money but with favors and respectful treatment. As such, he knew that they would never raise a finger against him no matter how much money Kolldehoff offered, or how much Lutz tried to intimidate them. They would simply avoid getting involved in the dispute altogether—which also meant they would avoid defending Kerrigan as well. They wouldn't side with him, but they also wouldn't side with his enemy. For this reason, the fourth day after his last two employees disappeared, Kerrigan knew for a fact that he would have to fight for his possessions on his own, and that the fight would be two against one.

"He spent the early part of the day loading every last weapon he had, one by one, and then he proceeded to place them in strategic locations throughout the building: next to every window (which he shattered with a thick wooden club) he placed a repeating rifle so that he could move about the building without being weighed down by a cumbersome weapon, secure in the knowledge that there would always be a firearm nearby. He also thought this would give Lutz and Kolldehoff the impression that he had several men inside the house firing at them, and while he didn't think this would necessarily deter them, he did think it would make them nervous and, most of all, wonder if they actually had an advantage over him. However, after he had calculated everything down to a science, so that there was nothing left to do but wait, the afternoon grew unbearable. Jittery, he paced through the empty rooms, tried unsuccessfully to concentrate on some reading material, and drank without pause. By the time night fell, he was in a high state of excitement, and somewhat inebriated to boot. Kerrigan's house was surrounded by bushes, and he watched over them from the window like a hawk. At around nine in the evening, he began to see shadows moving and began to hear footsteps in the dark, and at one point, he actually thought he saw the bushes move. At nine-thirty he heard a cry from somewhere off in the distance, and then he noticed an unusual glow by the port, which was barely visible from the offices of Kerrigan & Lutz. He paid little attention to this, however, and at ten o'clock, at which time he grew suspicious once again of the bushes down below, he heard Lutz's voice, which caught him by surprise. As the voice rang out, he turned off all the lights in the building.

"'Kerrigan! Your boats have been on fire for the last half hour; go out and take a look if you have the nerve!' the German yelled out.

"Kerrigan realized two things right then: first, that the glow he had noticed down by the port was, in fact, the glow of his boats on fire; and second, that Lutz had no interest in taking over the company. All he really wanted was to spite Kerrigan for the offer he had made the night of their one-year anniversary, and to this end he was willing to destroy whatever he had to: the ships, the cargo, the offices, everything. That was the moment Kerrigan realized that he had sorely miscalculated the defense of his properties and, furious at himself, responded by unleashing a burst of gunfire in the direction of Lutz's voice. As he heard Lutz fall back, looking for somewhere to hide in the bushes, several bullets pierced the shutters from where he had just fired. He moved away from the windows and waited a moment or two; it wasn't long before he heard Lutz's voice again.

"'You have nothing left, Kerrigan, just these bloody offices. Get out if you don't want to lose them, too—or else you'll go down with them. I've set fire to all the boats, but I know the money's still here. If you give us everything you have, we'll leave you alone.'

"Kerrigan fired once more at the bushes, but he could hear Lutz laughing even before the roar of the shots died down. He couldn't see a thing in that darkness, and his nerves were starting to take over. Suddenly he thought he heard a noise coming from the back door, ran over and emptied an entire round on the door. Then he thought he heard something creaking and when he opened the door to take a look, he was greeted with a spray of bullets, one of which hit him in the leg. It was, of course, Kolldehoff. Kerrigan quickly slammed the door, sank to the floor, and checked the bullet wound: it wasn't too severe, for the projectile hadn't hit any bones and he was still able to walk, so he tried to reassure himself with these thoughts. From outside, meanwhile, Lutz's voice continued to ring out, taunting and threatening him. Suddenly, Kerrigan thought of something. In a loud voice, he called out to Kolldehoff, who didn't respond, but Kerrigan went on talking anyway: 'I don't know who you are and I don't care, Kolldehoff, but I do know that you're a poor bastard who's flat broke—you don't have any money, not to buy my company, or even to catch the next boat back to Singapore. How much did Lutz pay you to do this? Whatever it was, I'll pay you triple if you'll help me catch Lutz. Let's finish him off, Kolldehoff. What do you say? Are you in?'

"After a few moments of silence, Kerrigan heard the Dutchman's terse reply, clear and precise.

"'No!' he shouted.

"Without skipping a beat, Lutz's voice rang out in triumph. First, he laughed: a big, long belly laugh and then he said, over and over again, that Kerrigan was through, a dead man. Once again, our captain ran toward the front door, and once again he fired at the bushes outside without success. A few minutes of silence followed, broken only by a loud gust of air that blew through the back of the house. Kerrigan ran toward the source of the noise and saw that Kolldehoff had thrown a burning torch through the window, the glass of which had already been fully blown away by the Dutchman's bullets. The curtains of what had once been his bedroom were now on fire; Kerrigan yanked them from their moorings and smothered the flames, but just as he extinguished the fire two more torches sailed through the broken window and Kerrigan heard Lutz toss more flaming torches inside the house. Kerrigan watched as one of them crashed down on the straw roof and sent flames throughout the house. That was when he remembered that he had a stockpile of gunpowder and ran to the room where he stored it. First he opened a window, tossed out three or four boxes—he didn't have time to dispose of any more because the smoke was starting to choke him and fill his eyes with tears, and because, right at that moment, he heard one of the two men attempting to break down the front door to the building. He quickly headed downstairs, limping somewhat from all the blood he had lost, and waited behind a massive wooden filing cabinet, with a pistol in either hand, for the front door to cave in. When it finally swung open, Kerrigan couldn't see anything until Lutz suddenly appeared, firing his gun every which way. Kerrigan waited a bit and only when he was certain that the smoke had penetrated Lutz's eyes and blinded them did he emerge from his hiding spot and open fire himself. Lutz dropped the shotgun he held and plummeted to the floor. In reality his fall was rather awkward, and within a few moments a reddish stain seeped into his straw-like blond hair and white suit. Kerrigan watched the man's features fade and then, as quickly as his wounded leg allowed, ran from the house, which he knew might explode at any minute, but as he raced toward the bushes he felt a bullet penetrate his left shoulder. He turned around just in time to see Kolldehoff, who had clearly entered the building through the front door that, until then, he had been guarding. One second later, all that remained of Kerrigan & Lutz exploded in the night air. To this day Kerrigan still does not know if, in fact, Kolldehoff actually died. The authorities eventually located Lutz's feet and part of his thorax, but they never found a shred of evidence to prove that the silent Dutchman had been blown to bits that night. Of course, nobody ever heard from him again, either.

"Now, as I said at the very beginning of this story, in 1892 Kerrigan was living in the city of Amoy, bankrupt, prematurely aging, desolate, and filled with rage. He had pinned all his hopes on his plan to start anew and live a tranquil, easy existence as the head of his shipping outfit, which had taken him a full five years to get off the ground. The obliteration of everything he possessed, including all his money, came as a terrible blow and left him even more bitter and cynical than he had been before. Convinced that nothing mattered anymore and knowing that he no longer stood the slightest chance of becoming an honorable, decent gentleman, he decided that his only solution was to live for and in the present moment, with no consideration for anyone else. You may wonder how I can possibly state with conviction that this was the moment Kerrigan came to this realization, and all I can say is that Kerrigan always harbored a secret desire to give up his itinerant, adventurous life and become the kind of man his father had been: a landowner adored and admired by his family and neighbors. If Kerrigan turned into a tough, cruel, ruthless man it was mainly due to the terribly tragic circumstances in which he had found himself. As I said, he had his change of heart around the year 1892, only twelve years ago, a fact that only makes him nobler, for the person he is today has little or nothing to do with the man he was

118

twelve years ago. After all, it is not so easy for such a disillusioned man to turn around and change his life—especially for someone like Kerrigan, who was already past forty at that point. But he did it, believe me, despite the fact that he threw Amanda Cook overboard and stabbed Captain Seebohm a few days ago. I myself shot Léonide Meffre just a few days ago, and I don't think that makes me a depraved man, despite what Miss Bonington may think. Very well, let me continue with my tale: Captain Kerrigan managed to get himself to Hong Kong, and he stayed there, wandering around the docks and doing odd jobs here and there. Once he had fully recovered from all the wounds he had sustained that fateful night, he tried to get himself hired as a crew member on one of the boats headed for America, though this was much harder than it seemed: Kerrigan wanted to go home precisely during one of the most massive waves of emigration to the great American continent, and he found himself among thousands upon thousands of Asians who wanted exactly what he did. Neither his experience nor his status as an American were of any use to him, and in addition—this is highly confidential—his rank of captain was pure fiction. Leaving China became such an obsession that he actually murdered two sailors, one American, one French, in the hopes of assuming their identities after making off with their identification and uniforms. But on both occasions—in the first case because the victim turned out to be the son of his ship's captain, and the other because Kerrigan's knowledge of French was skimpy at best—his crimes were discovered, and he was forced to flee in a terrible hurry both times and had to remain undercover until the ships of both his victims had set sail. His situation was so desperate that on one occasion he actually tried to hang himself, only to be saved at the very last minute by someone whose name I cannot remember. And so he plodded along like this, his miserable existence marked by one setback after another, until the opportunity to leave Hong Kong for good finally and rather unexpectedly fell in his lap. Kerrigan,

JAVIER MARÍAS

among many other vocational pursuits, had become an able and
wily purse-snatcher, and for a time following the demise of
Kerrigan & Lutz, he practiced this craft quite assiduously, and was
a frequent visitor to the lobbies of all the great hotels in the city.
He had managed to hang on to one of his elegant suits and a pair
of resplendent boots from his days as the president of a shipping
company, and in this outfit, topped off with a recently stolen hat,
he blended in perfectly at all these grand hotels, and was never
once asked to leave by a single doorman, manager, or porter. His
exploits, never terribly spectacular, usually went undetected and
unreported until he was long gone, and so his face was never identified nor were his movements monitored by the detectives that
worked at such hotels. In addition, the people who usually paid
the price for this type of petty larceny were the local porters and
bellhops, which meant that Kerrigan was able to enjoy almost total
impunity in his life as a small-time crook. One day, then, he found
himself sitting on a sofa in the vestibule of the Hotel Empire, perhaps the second-finest lodging in the city, when he noticed a for-
midable, impeccably dressed gentleman with a carefully tended
moustache and monumental monocle sitting beside him. From the
impatient, testy air he gave off, Kerrigan deduced that the man,
who looked to be in his fifties, was awaiting the arrival of a lady
who had lingered a bit too long in her dressing room. As Kerrigan
idly skimmed the pages of a newspaper his hand crept toward the
right-hand pocket of the gentleman's jacket with surprising
alacrity—emboldened, no doubt, by his well-honed talent—and
then he slipped it into the gentleman's pocket. Patting about ever
so lightly, he finally made contact with the item he sought and just
as he very slowly removed a leather billfold, using only his index
and middle fingers, the gentleman stood up to acknowledge the
arrival of a young man, who was also extremely well-dressed.
Kerrigan had just enough time to hide it undetected: not a second
after the billfold was safely out of sight, the gentleman turned to

120

Kerrigan and asked him if he would mind moving over a bit to make room for his friend. Kerrigan very solicitously obliged, and the two men began talking. The older man was in a foul mood for two reasons: his wife was unforgivably late—Kerrigan's instinct, sharp as always, had not failed him—and his attempts to hire an expert sailor had been completely fruitless. The young man, perhaps only a few years younger than Kerrigan, who was about forty at the time, replied that he too had been unsuccessful and blamed it on the fact that all the sailors insisted on receiving their wages in advance. The gentleman with the monocle very rudely snapped back at the young man, telling him that he didn't know what he was talking about: times had simply changed, and there were fewer people out there who were willing to take risks. According to the older man, the sailors in the city of Amoy were all a bunch of cowards who wouldn't budge an inch unless they knew exactly where they were going and precisely how long their journey would last. He knew his plans were rather eccentric, but the local sailors' doubts and fears seemed excessive to him. As you might have guessed by now, Kerrigan acted swiftly and decisively. The conversation offered no details whatsoever regarding the nature of the journey the two men were planning, but he couldn't be bothered with details—it didn't really matter as long as it got him out of China, where bad luck seemed to plague him at every turn, no matter where he went or what he did. And so, after waiting until the monocled gentleman had fully turned to face his companion, Kerrigan pulled out the billfold he had just stolen, touched the gentleman lightly on the shoulder and offered it to him, claiming that it had just fallen to the floor. The gentleman, who must have been in a truly dismal mood indeed, did not even bother patting his own pocket and, glancing at Kerrigan with disdain, asked him if he was certain the billfold was his. Kerrigan replied affirmatively, using the language used by sailors of the British Navy. 'Aye aye, sir,' he said, and explained that he had seen it slide from the gentleman's jacket pocket following a sharp arm movement. As you well know, the very idiosyncratic argot that sailors employ instead of simply saying 'yes' is known throughout the world but on this particular occasion the two gentlemen in question happened to be Englishmen living in India, and when they heard Kerrigan's response their faces suddenly lit up, and the older man, even before accepting his billfold, immediately asked him if he was a sailor.

"'Aye, aye, sir,' Kerrigan repeated, in an exaggeratedly British accent. 'For fifteen years I served as the captain of a ship that sailed under the British crown.' And then he added: 'Captain Joseph Dunhill Kerrigan, at your service.'

"The monocled gentleman finally accepted his billfold, said thank you to Kerrigan, and introduced himself as Dr. Horace Merivale. Right away the younger man followed suit and introduced himself as Reginald Holland, and both, almost in unison, asked him if he would like to have a drink with them at the hotel. Kerrigan politely accepted the invitation, and the three men walked over to the bar, though not before alerting the concierge to please send Mrs. Merivale over to them when she came downstairs. Once they had sat down and their drinks had been served, Reginald Holland ventured to ask Kerrigan if he was still in active service, but before Kerrigan could reply that he was retired and only in Hong Kong on vacation—which he did get to squeeze in a bit later on—Dr. Merivale cut him off, declaring that the one thing he demanded of all his conversations and interactions, whether personal or professional, was honesty, and he scolded Holland for beating around the bush. Then he turned to face Kerrigan head-on and explained very clearly that they urgently required the services of someone who was intimately familiar with the secrets of the high seas and who was willing to set sail for the Pacific Ocean in no specific direction, solely to search for heavenly islands. Kerrigan, somewhat taken aback by this proposal, asked him exactly what he meant by 'heavenly islands.' Dr. Merivale blushed slightly, perhaps thinking that Kerrigan had taken him for an innocent, and clarified: both he and Holland were exceedingly wealthy men—he did not mention the source of their riches, but Kerrigan assumed that they had inherited either mines or the controlling interest in major businesses—and their intention was to purchase an uninhabited island in the Pacific where the sun shone all year long, all this at the behest of the capricious Mrs. Merivale, of course. Once they found their island they would build a grand mansion or, who knew, perhaps they would even found a city which would be exclusively of their possession and which they might even baptize with the name of Merry Holland—at this, the younger man blushed even more, though whether out of embarrassment or pleasure I cannot say. Merivale added that they had of course declined to tell this story to the uncouth Chinese sailors they had come across, sensing that they were people of dull wits and few scruples who would have only laughed at their intentions or tried to rob them blind at the earliest opportunity. With the Chinese, Merivale and Holland had concocted a story about being archeologists in search of uncharted islands. Then he quickly added, with a kind of grandiose obsequiousness, that of course things were different now that they were in the presence of an esteemed sailor from the British Navy, a man of the world who understood the complexities of life, an honorable officer of the Crown. Kerrigan, who listened to these two megalomaniacs with a truly British, steely indifference, simply replied that he accepted their offer, declared that the salary was of no consequence—he even invited them to name the amount—and then inquired as to whether they already possessed a proper sailing vessel. The two men, thrilled at his reply, responded that they had already acquired, for a reasonable price considering that the boat had plenty of amenities, a small sailboat that lacked nothing but a captain—whom they had just hired—and two sailors—whom they imagined Kerrigan would have little trouble recruiting from the legions of brutes they saw wandering through the streets every day. With that, they shook Kerrigan's hand firmly and warmly.

"Kerrigan asked if he might inspect the boat before they left the port and promised he would have it ready for sailing within thirty-six hours, complete with the two brutes. Dr. Merivale and Mr. Holland laughed with amusement at Kerrigan's turn of phrase, such an ingenious way of referring to the two men who would be, in effect, their travel companions. They then settled the bar bill, though not before arranging to meet Kerrigan the following day so that the captain could check the condition of the boat, to ensure that it was in fact adequate for their very extravagant purposes, and at the same time study the route they would be taking and offer his advice to that end. With that, the men retired, no doubt to see Mrs. Merivale and tell her of their news.

"The *Uttaradit* was a fishing boat; to describe it in any detail would be superfluous. The point is, it set sail seventy-two hours after this conversation took place, with six people on board as planned. Contrary to what one might have expected, the two megalomaniacs and Mrs. Merivale, as soon as they had abandoned the port of Hong Kong and found themselves truly deprived of all contact—the kind that grows indispensable out of habit—with subordinates waiting to serve them hand and foot, immediately and completely lost whatever interest they ever had in knowing the sailboat's route, and from that point forward virtually stopped speaking to Kerrigan altogether. True representatives of a society—much like our own—that conceives of existence as nothing more than a voyage along the horizon, free of obstacles and bumps, that one embarks upon for the sole purpose of contemplation, these people left absolutely everything in Kerrigan's hands—not just the affairs and management of the boat itself but all the details of their very ambitious enterprise. This did not displease Kerrigan at all—on the contrary, in fact. Given that Merivale and Holland were on a quest to find an island that enjoyed a

permanently balmy climate, the sailboat had to head south, because the Pacific islands situated along the same parallel as Hong
Kong, aside from being very few and far between, are not blessed
by such pleasant temperatures. But as I have already mentioned,
Kerrigan wanted nothing more than to return to his native land,
so after steering the boat in a southerly direction for a few days,
and also after confirming that his employers were both trusting
and ignorant, he took a sharp turn in the direction that Merivale
and Holland, had they ever once stopped to think that the sun
rises in the east, should have easily identified as easterly. The
brutes, of course, made it clear that they knew precisely where
they were headed but did not dare argue with their captain. Kerrigan, it seems, made the decision to deceive his employers without having first configured a plan that would allow him to escape,
unscathed, the ire that he would most certainly inspire in these ec-
centrics once they realized—and sooner or later they would have
to realize—how very gravely he had taken advantage of their in-
nocence. But he didn't care. Given that the two men were terribly busy laying out in the sun, coddling their stomachs against the
rocking of the ship, and playing bridge in their cabins, Kerrigan
calculated that the gentlemen would not catch on to what he had
done until, at the very earliest, they had reached the Brooks
Islands, and by then, Kerrigan figured—or rather, he knew—he
would have worked up either a feasible plan or the necessary valor
to put an end to these people without further ado.

"Mrs. Merivale, whose first name was Beatrice, was another
story. Blond, very beautiful, capricious, and arrogant, she seemed to
scorn all of humanity, including her own husband and Mr. Holland.
Much younger than her spouse, whom she had no doubt married
for his money, she wore wide-legged white pants, scarves knotted
at the neck, and blouses with the first three buttons undone, exud-
ing an aura that was a cross between absent and provocative as she
strolled about the boat, or else spent long hours sitting beside

Kerrigan, distracting him with her fragrance. Very occasionally, she would also distract him with idle questions about the ocean or the finer points of navigation, always formulated in a tone that, more than anything, seemed to suggest that she considered Kerrigan nothing more than a manual designed to supply her with answers to all her questions. This, along with her habit of combing her long blond hair on deck, only served to exasperate Kerrigan, who felt unable to initiate any kind of advance or insinuation with respect to her. She did not seem to be a foolish woman—the opposite, in fact, and for this reason, while the captain was certain that neither of the two men had realized his abrupt change of direction, he had no idea whether Beatrice Merivale was aware of what he had done. Sometimes, while her husband and Reginald Holland were immersed in their card games, she would gaze at Kerrigan for long periods of time, as if she were silently asking him to explain his decision not to obey orders, and this left Kerrigan bewildered, unsure of the intention behind the defiant look on her face. When, after ten days on the high seas, the two gentlemen asked Kerrigan why they had not encountered any islands along their route and Mrs. Merivale very calmly replied, in a tone that chided them ever so slightly for their ignorance, that the *Uttaradit* was not the kind of boat they were accustomed to—they normally traveled on those modern steamships that advanced rapidly through the water— Kerrigan began to suspect that, albeit tacitly, Beatrice Merivale had succumbed to his will.

"The days went by, and Kerrigan, eminently aware that the two gentlemen who had hired him might very well be as impatient as they were innocent, changed his mind and altered his plans. First, he slowed the boat down from the rapid pace at which they had previously been sailing, and then he called a meeting with the sailboat's three passengers to announce that they were now approaching an archipelago. Dr. Merivale and Reginald Holland received the news with tremendous glee, while Mrs.

Merivale responded with a puzzled expression that only confirmed the captain's suspicions. Kerrigan had decided to drop
anchor at Marcus Island, which boasted countless ancillary islets
that did not appear on any maps and which could, in some way,
be construed as 'uncharted'—in part to placate his employers but
also because he had noticed that they were beginning to run low
on certain provisions and he felt that the Uttaradit, a rather inappropriate vessel for the long-distance enterprise to be undertaken,
ought to be inspected at port, or perhaps even exchanged for
another, larger vessel. The millionaires, however, were so delighted by the prospect of visiting one of these deserted islands that,
despite the fictitious malfunction Kerrigan had dreamed up to
force them to stop first at the main—and already inhabited—
island in search of a mechanic, they urged him, if at all possible, to
first visit these islands that were, to them, potential possessions.
Kerrigan, who did not want to arouse their ire under any circumstances, had no choice but to comply with their wishes. And so he
turned the sailboat in the direction of the islets, some one hundred
miles to the south of Marcus Island, somewhat flustered by the
infantile cheers proffered by Merivale and Holland. After spending
the rest of the morning on a small, ugly island that held absolutely no appeal for them, the enthusiasm among the group had sub-
sided considerably. Finally, tired and slightly disillusioned, they set
off for the main island. Marcus Island, or Minamitorijima to the
Japanese, is a triangular elevated atoll perched at twenty meters
above sea level, and is surrounded on all sides by coral reefs.
According to Kerrigan, the port was pathetic, and the number of
boats anchored there could be counted on a single hand. The
Uttaradit was the strongest and fastest of them all, in fact, which
dashed Kerrigan's hopes of exchanging it for a more powerful vessel. All the island had was one tiny fishing village with some twenty inhabitants, and a single commercial establishment that served as
both a supply store and canteen. There, they were able to purchase

provisions and a few trinkets—hats, shawls, beads—that Merivale and Holland found exotic. Kerrigan then suggested they spend the night there and wait for their brutes who, along with an Austrian mechanic they encountered on the island, would fix the damaged sailboat so that they might set off the following day in search of their paradise islands. As the *Uttaradit* was inspected that evening, the captain and his passengers waited in the canteen. Sitting down at the one and only table in the place, they asked the gentleman in charge if he happened to have any wine. If not for the Austrian mechanic, who turned up shortly thereafter, told them nothing at all was amiss with their boat, and then immediately invited himself to join them, Kerrigan would have gotten the doctor and his friend drunk and departed with Mrs. Merivale as his sole passenger. But the Austrian mechanic, who was living in that godforsaken place for reasons they could scarcely begin to imagine, ruined Kerrigan's plans. He was a coarse, talkative man with a protruding belly, an immense bluish black moustache, a perfectly awful English accent, and a repulsive last name: Flock. He reacted with— perhaps overstated—shock to Kerrigan's claim that the small Chinese sailboat was in disrepair, and drank far more than he should have, which prevented Merivale and Holland from doing the same, and he then proceeded to interrogate Mrs. Merivale with an intensity that was far from appropriate. Kerrigan, annoyed by all this, did not utter a single word as they sat and drank inside that ramshackle establishment. There was, however, a moment when he felt an almost irresistible impulse to punch Flock in the face, and he had to bite his lips to refrain from doing so. Beatrice responded to the Austrian's distasteful questions with little more than monosyllables, but the megalomaniacs, in part to keep Flock from talking so much to the lady, and in part because they had recovered their optimism and good humor thanks to the wine they had begun to swill, began to talk about their travels more freely than they should have, and ended up telling the Austrian mechanic the reasons that led them to such an unusual destination. At that point Flock, who was probably a decent fellow who meant no harm at all, suddenly exclaimed, in surprise: 'Oh, but to do that you have to go farther south! You won't find anything here to your liking.'

"'Farther south?' Holland inquired, and added, 'At what parallel is this island?'

"At that moment, Kerrigan was about ready to pounce on Flock, but he had to hold back as Flock replied: 'We're a bit farther north, almost at the Tropic of Cancer.'

"Merivale turned to face Kerrigan and asked him how this could possibly be true. The captain, somewhat nervous, replied that he had changed direction without consulting them for their own good: he was an expert in this particular part of the Pacific, and knew of several islands very close by that would satisfy all their requirements. However, they had been so adamant about traveling south that he hadn't dared to tell them anything, fearful that they would grow angry and force him to turn around before they arrived. Once they laid eyes on these islands, Kerrigan said, he was certain they would thank him for taking such an initiative. At that point Flock, seconded by the millionaires, who suddenly recalled the disappointment they had felt earlier that morning upon visiting that first islet, told him he had to be mistaken. Flock assured the group that he knew the area extremely well, and said he was absolutely certain that the islands to be found nearby were in no way comparable to the ones that lay farther to the south, in the Carolinas, and he advised them to head in that direction. Kerrigan, tenacious as ever, refuted the Austrian's comments by claiming, in an extremely offended tone of voice, that he knew exactly what he was doing and added that he never would have changed course had he not been absolutely convinced that the islets around Marcus Island were the most beautiful to be found in all the Pacific Ocean. At that, Flock let out a cackle which led them into

an endless discussion on the topic. Over and over again, he promised them that there was no way they would ever find anything of
interest in that area, and Kerrigan, who was growing more agitated
by the second, continued to defend his claims. The millionaires refrained from saying much aside from remarking that, in fact, the
island they had seen that morning fell far short of Kerrigan's praise
and seemed to support Flock's argument. Things went on like this
for about half an hour until, all of a sudden, Beatrice Merivale
clapped her hand against the table and called out: 'Enough is
enough, gentlemen. Now, whom would you rather believe? A miserable boat mechanic who, as we can all see, has never amounted
to much of anything?' she asked, looking Flock up and down with
infinite scorn. 'Or a captain at the service of the Crown, who has
already proven himself to be an expert at his craft, a man who
enjoys a respectable position in society and who obviously has a
brilliant professional record that modesty prevents him from brag-
ging about, and who has been generous enough to accept our
unusual offer when we were desperate and his plans were quite
different indeed? I can hardly believe, gentlemen, that you would
doubt, even for a second, which of these men is telling the truth.'

"Merivale and Holland fell silent and looked at each other
sheepishly. After a few more seconds of silence, Kerrigan found it
a convenient moment to intervene: 'Thank you, Mrs. Merivale,' he
said. 'I appreciate your words of support. Gentlemen, if you so
wish, we can depart tomorrow morning for the Carolinas. I do not
blame you for questioning why I brought you here without your
permission but please, believe me, I did so for the reasons I just
mentioned, and I do think that no matter what, now that we are
here, you have nothing to lose by taking the morning to visit the
nearby islets. Did you really think you would want to acquire the
first island you laid eyes on? Had that been the case, you certainly
wouldn't have required my services. I must ask you to trust me,
and I promise you that if by tomorrow you are not satisfied with

what you find then of course we will immediately change direction and sail toward the Carolinas.'

"Merivale and Holland turned to look at one another again. Merivale then said he would agree to Kerrigan's proposal and, along with Holland, apologized to Kerrigan for having doubted his expertise and his integrity. Flock, who had said nothing, and probably felt quite humiliated, since Beatrice Merivale had pounded her fist against the table so forcefully, suddenly stood up, removed a slip of paper from his frayed jacket pocket, and handed it to Reginald Holland.

"'As you prefer,' he said, very casually. 'It's your business, after all. But at least allow me to give you this map of Marcus Island and the vicinity; I drew it up myself. Follow it carefully: do not miss a single one of the islands I include. Examine them for yourselves and you will no doubt have a better opinion of Dieter Flock. That will prove to you that I am the one who is in the right.'

"Holland grabbed the map, unfolded it, glanced at it, and handed it over to Kerrigan, not without allowing Dr. Merivale to take a look over his shoulder first. Kerrigan placed it in the upper pocket of his jacket. Dieter Flock, his head hanging down, left the establishment, and five minutes later Kerrigan, Reginald Holland, and the Merivales did the same. They walked back to the *Uttaradit* and, after bidding one another good night, retired to their respective cabins to rest up from the very exhausting day they had had.

"As you can see, Mr. Bayham, things started to get complicated: not just because it had been extremely misguided of Kerrigan to think that he could keep the peace on board until they reached the Brooks Islands, but because destiny had, as she often does, come into play in a most unusual way.

"The following day, Kerrigan awoke to the very unpleasant surprise that the two Chinese brutes had disappeared. Kerrigan interrogated the townspeople to find out where they might have gone, but it was none other than Flock who, at the door to the supply shop, and with an insolence that was well-tinged with rancor, remarked that he had seen them leave in some kind of canoe before dawn, and he assured them that there was no way they would find, at least not on Marcus Island, any sailors who would be willing to replace them. And he was exactly right: Kerrigan had no other choice but to set sail without a crew—that is, without any crew other than Dr. Merivale and Mr. Holland, upon whom he impressed the gravity of the situation before forcing them to unfurl sails, climb ladders, and take over the helm on occasion, always under his guidance, of course. Kerrigan had spent the entire night racking his brains to figure out how he could prove that he and not Flock had been right. He was entirely unfamiliar with the area, and he was convinced that the Austrian's map—a conscientious effort that was clearly the work of someone who knew plenty about cartography—was completely accurate and that the beauty of the islets near Marcus Island was a figment of his imagination. With this in mind, he decided that the best thing to do would be to head as quickly as possible for the Mariana Islands, where the climate was far more forgiving and the geography far more heavenly than that of Marcus Island, and convince the millionaires that the Marianas were in fact the Marcus Islands, a ruse he was certain they would never detect, for he would explain that a fast-approaching typhoon had forced him to take an extremely circuitous route, which would explain why it took them so much longer to reach the outlying islands this time around. Of course, he was right: they believed everything he said, with the exception, no doubt, of Beatrice Merivale, who by then had become Captain Kerrigan's staunchest ally, as she had indicated during her intervention in the dispute with Dieter Flock. Kerrigan grew more and more certain of this, but Mrs. Merivale's combination of intransigence and passivity kept him uncertain and in suspense, and for this reason he did not venture to make any bold moves just in case his hunch was unfounded. What Kerrigan failed to realize—in the end, he had little or no intuition when it came to women—was that Beatrice Merivale belonged to that class of females who, being victims of shyness, too little affection, and a pattern of having someone else make their decisions for them, never ask for things directly no matter how ardent their desires, and always wait for others to take the initiative.

"I don't know what kind of magic Kerrigan must have spun with his improvised crew—well, don't take my word for it; I know nothing about sailing, and perhaps I am not repeating precisely what our ill-fated captain told me with regard to dates and times—but from what I believe he said, the Mariana Islands came into view toward the end of the following morning. Dr. Merivale and Reginald Holland, men for whom sentiments such as disappointment and skepticism did not exist—were as enthused as ever by the sights that now unfolded before their eyes. As such, they redoubled their efforts, and in less than an hour they disembarked on an island that looked as if it just might meet all of their requirements for becoming the future city of Merry Holland. The two men quickly prepared to explore the small landmass as soon as they had finished helping Kerrigan successfully bring the vessel ashore, and invited Beatrice and the captain to join them. Beatrice, however, declined, replying that she was not interested and that she trusted her husband's good judgment. Kerrigan did the same, claiming he wished to review the malfunction that Flock had been unable to identify, because he still noticed it whenever they sailed above a certain speed. And so the two megalomaniacs, especially giddy because they had a feeling that this island was going to be just what they were looking for, set off through the tropical underbrush on their own, giving Kerrigan and Mrs. Merivale their very first opportunity to be alone together.

"By the time they returned at nightfall, Kerrigan had already seduced Mrs. Merivale—or, if you prefer, Mrs. Merivale had already seduced Kerrigan. As I mentioned before, Mr. Bayham, it was fate, disguised as Dieter Flock, that precipitated things: Dr. Horace Merivale and his friend Reginald returned from their expedition so overjoyed that they did not realize what had happened in their absence, even though Kerrigan's very deep feelings of tenderness were clearly visible on his face. Jubilant, they announced to Kerrigan and Mrs. Merivale that they had decided to purchase the island and that they would set sail for Hong Kong the following day to take care of all the legal details required to effect the acquisition. Just as he had previously experienced with his partner Lutz, Kerrigan was taken very much aback by the one thing he hadn't planned for. Rapidly he weighed the possibilities: he could maintain his charade and lead them to believe that he was bringing them back to the Chinese port while secretly setting sail for San Francisco, but then, just as he had done when Lutz and Kolldehoff had presented their counteroffer, he decided to stop anticipating or avoiding possible eventualities, and face up to the present moment. It was one thing for Merivale and Holland not to realize that they were going northwest when they should have been going southeast, but it was quite a stretch—rather impossible, he admitted—to hope that they would not realize they were heading west when they were supposed to be heading east. And while it might have been very characteristic of Kerrigan to give up the fight after having indefatigably and successfully evaded a host of perilous and devilishly complicated situations, I do think that on this particular occasion the existence of Beatrice Merivale influenced his resolve, and the next thing Kerrigan did was remove a pistol from the right-hand pocket of his jacket and point it at his employers. At first, Merivale and Holland thought it was a joke, and Holland even told him to please point it the other way, but when Kerrigan fired a bullet into the sand, the two men jumped up with a start, furrowed their brows, and waited for the captain to speak.

"'The two of you aren't going anywhere,' he said. 'You are going to stay right here, on this island you love so much. I need the *Uttaradit* to get to Luzón, and from there get a ticket to San Francisco with the money you owe me.'

"The two gentlemen didn't quite understand what Kerrigan was talking about, but they did find it odd that he had suddenly lost his strong British accent and clipped pronunciation, replacing it with a torrent of unambiguously low-class American slang. Seeing that this was no laughing matter, the two men refrained from asking any further questions and simply tried to reason with him, telling him that there was no need to pull a gun on them to get what he wanted—they could all travel together to Hong Kong, where Kerrigan could buy a first-class ticket to San Francisco. They assured him that they intended to pay him a fabulous amount of money for the services he had rendered, and that he would have everything he wanted once they reached Hong Kong. Kerrigan, as he himself admits, had second thoughts. As you have surely noticed during the course of this story, he had more scruples than even he himself realized. He would have had no trouble at all robbing and murdering his passengers the day they departed for Hong Kong, and yet he chose not to do so. He could have kept them at bay and forced them to obey his orders when Flock revealed that they were much farther north than they had imagined, but he demurred. Instead he tried his best to keep up appearances and cause them as little harm as possible. The benevolence with which he treated those two imbeciles was altogether admirable. Kerrigan, despite his tough exterior, was not a man who felt terribly sure of himself. For this reason, a wave of doubt came over him when Dr. Horace Merivale and Reginald Holland tried to reason with him. He turned to Beatrice, and looked in her eyes for an answer. She nodded ever so slightly.

"'But there is another matter we must address, Dr. Merivale,' Kerrigan said. 'Your wife wishes to come with me. What do you say to that? I have no choice but to leave you here, though I am sorry to have to do it. I feel no ill will toward you.'

"Dr. Merivale suddenly understood what had happened in his absence, and his long face twisted into a grimace of pure bile. His eyes first settled on his wife, and then traveled over to Kerrigan, and then, without any warning, he lifted his sharpened cane until it was horizontal, and he lunged at the captain, striking him in the torso. Having failed, at least partially, to achieve his real goal, Dr. Merivale lost his balance and fell facedown on the ground with his back to Kerrigan, who quickly got up and shot the doctor in the neck just as he had begun to pick himself up off the ground. Merivale had barely enough time to hear the tiny bones in his head splinter apart, and once again he fell flat on his face, though this time it was because he was dead. Reginald Holland, in a fit of hysteria from what he had just witnessed, pounced on the captain and knocked him to the ground with a single blow. Kerrigan, shocked, sustained the fall, and Holland ran to the boat, which was anchored just a few meters away and quickly entered one of the cabins, only to emerge a few seconds later with a rifle in his hands. Standing on the upper deck of the *Uttaradit,* he pointed his weapon at Kerrigan, but the captain had already jumped to his feet and was waiting for him with his right arm extended and in position. He fired four times before Holland could even pull his trigger. The bullet he shot careened into the fine sand on the beach, and Holland fell into the water close to the shore, his shirt already soaked with blood.

"What comes next is another story entirely. An *affaire d'amour* was what finally led Kerrigan to radically change his way of life. That is all I shall say about it, because I have never known quite how to talk about love—that much you surely know about me if you have ever read any of my novels. You must have heard as much. Kerrigan may be a man of very refined sensibilities, but I simply can-

not bring myself to do it; I would only end up using the most typical clichés; I just do not know how to talk of such things. All
I will tell you is that their story was a very lovely one indeed.

"As soon as they finished burying the bodies of Merivale and
Holland they did nothing but bask in the glow of one another on
that island until their provisions ran out. Forgive me for being
prosaic, but I cannot help it. Beatrice Merivale did belong to the
class of females I previously described; she also happened to be a
sensual, seductive woman who knew how to love a man. From
beneath her icy veneer, all kinds of impassioned, insatiable feelings
bubbled up to the surface. And she made a happy man of Kerrigan,
who had never before found the time to fall in love. They
remained on the island that would never be called Merry Holland
for a month, after which time they started up the *Uttaradit* and
returned to Hong Kong. From there they took the train to Jam-
shedpur, a city where Beatrice, her husband, and Holland had lived
for a time. Beatrice inherited Dr. Merivale's fortune, and after a
few months she and Kerrigan were married. After settling down
in San Francisco—yes, the second in command of the *Tallahassee*
finally made it to the great city in California—they bought the
island, which to this day has no name. They often spent long
stretches of time there, living in a house they built together, and
they had more money than they could ever possibly dream of
spending. Now you know the nature of Kerrigan's fortune, which
allowed him to give up his wanderlust, for he had finally achieved
his old goal of becoming immensely rich. And though it is a beautiful story, it is also rather commonplace, and I am sorry that it has
to end there: I would have preferred the episode with Lutz to have
come later—I like that part much better. I neglected to mention
that their version of how Merivale and Holland met their death
was rather imaginative: as far as the rest of the world was concerned, those two luckless devils died as heroes. Two men battling
the elements, fighting a powerful storm in the Pacific Ocean, their

bodies thrown to the sea by the turbulent waters.

"As I said, Kerrigan and Beatrice were married, but after four years' time she died quite tragically in a train crash near San Francisco, on her way back to Kerrigan following a brief separation. He was never the same after that. He never recovered from this blow, and every so often he is overcome by such terrible, overwhelming grief that he can scarcely bear the pain. The only way he knows how to endure these moments of crisis is by abandoning everything and spending a period of time on their island. Nobody else has ever set foot on it, with the exception, of course, of Dr. Merivale and Mr. Holland, whose mortal remains will lie there for all eternity. There, his memories come alive again, and instead of breaking his heart all over again, they have a calming effect on his soul.

"I had only the most general idea of what had happened until a few days ago, when Kerrigan told me the entire story in detail. Right in the middle of the expedition he suddenly found himself in the throes of one of these bouts of melancholy, and that was why he got so violently drunk—because he couldn't bear the idea of being stuck on board the *Tallahassee,* unable to return to his island. And while it may be true that he endangered the lives of Miss Cook, Captain Seebohm, and Miss Bonington, it was only because he was totally distraught; he didn't know what he was doing, though he never, at any moment, intended to hurt anyone. That was why he asked me to tell you everything and to apologize to all of you on his behalf. And yes, I am truly relieved Miss Bonington was not able to hear the story. I believe it might be a bit much for the sensibilities of a woman as delicate as she seems to be. For the moment, all I can say is that the episode is behind us now and Captain Kerrigan is once again behaving like a gentleman. I hope you believe me, because it is the truth, and I also hope that what I have just told you has changed your opinion of him somewhat. You know, I did tell him about some of the terrible things he did,

138

but I would also like to think I was wise enough to omit certain details that revealed him to be not an unscrupulous boor but simply a man whose past had come back to haunt him under some very extreme circumstances. And you know, Reginald Holland was the very last man Kerrigan ever killed. Now that I think of it, I realize that before today I never really spoke to him about how much he changed after falling in love with Beatrice Merivale. It happened gradually, and the proof, I believe, is that we have never seen him behave with the kind of spite he unleashed on Lutz, Kolldehoff, Merivale, and Holland. After he fell in love with Beatrice, he became another man. I never even really touched on the subject with him because, as I said before, I have never been able to say anything intelligent about love, although perhaps it would behoove me to learn how. I know plenty of writers who write the most eloquent and unforgettable passages on the subject, but me, I blush at the mere thought of it. I haven't ever been able to do it, not even with the women I have loved. I—"

Victor Arledge stopped himself at that point. A look of displeasure came over his face as he consulted his watch and realized that a great deal of time had gone by. Rising up from his chair, he studied his image in the mirror hanging above the armoire in his cabin, smoothed out his hair, and straightened his tie. Grabbing his cane, he started to walk toward the dining room in the hope that it wasn't too late to get something to eat.

BOOK SIX

T hings worsened considerably when everyone found out that Kerrigan had killed Eugene Collins, the boatswain. Fordington-Lewthwaite, an ambitious man whose goal was to become the captain and commander of his own ship no matter what steps he had to climb on the proverbial ladder of influence, had not been satisfied with the original explanation for Collins's death back when he was just an underling, even though everyone else—including Colonel McLiam and the British Police in Alexandria—had more or less accepted the story, and once he finally assumed his position as the de facto captain of the ship, he believed he would be duly rewarded if he got to the bottom of the matter. Guided by his simple intuition, he decided that a man as violent as Kerrigan—whom he would have otherwise regarded as nothing but a drunken lout had it not been for the Amanda Cook incident—necessarily had to have been involved in the boatswain's disappearance. Plus, it was known that the boatswain, an argumentative, aggressive man, did not get along very well with the second in command of the *Tallahassee*. Fordington-Lewthwaite, fully aware that the passengers—whom he treated with a deference bordering on servility—now thought the very worst of Kerrigan, knew that they would never utter a word in protest if he were to declare Kerrigan guilty of murdering Collins. And so, a week after the body of Léonide Meffre had been thrown into the waters of the Mediterranean, Fordington-Lewthwaite recruited two volunteers to go with him to Kerrigan's cabin. Victor Arledge and Lederer Tourneur watched on, rather perplexed, as the three men very purposefully entered the room and locked the door behind them, and waited around until they emerged. Fordington-Lewthwaite and his underlings remained inside for an hour, during which time the two writers grew quite alarmed as they listened to the sound of punches and cries coming out from behind the closed door, but they did not dare try to break in. When he finally emerged, Fordington-Lewthwaite was sweating profusely through his shirtsleeves with a look of satisfaction on his face. Arledge and Tourneur followed the smug, self-satisfied sailor as he walked out, and stared him down until he finally told them that Kerrigan had confessed to the murder of Collins.

It appeared that Fordington-Lewthwaite had been right after all, and though his decision had been arbitrary and his methods far from legitimate, his intuition had not failed him in this case. As it turned out, Kerrigan and Collins had gotten into a heated discussion regarding the way Collins treated his subordinates, and the argument had come to blows. Collins had pulled out a dagger, and Kerrigan, apparently in self-defense—though Fordington-Lewthwaite very astutely failed to mention this—had cut Collins's throat with one of the thick ropes that, rolled up in spirals, lay all over the deck of the *Tallahassee*. What happened next, however, was the basis for Fordington-Lewthwaite's murder accusation: Kerrigan apparently finished off the job by firing a shot—point-blank, which explained why nobody had heard the blast—into the boatswain's occipital lobe and dragging his body across the deck, very slowly and carefully to make sure that nobody would hear the sound of his body (in a truly grotesque position on top of one of the coils of rope and propped up by a couple of tackles) as it made contact with the water. Though Arledge's first reaction was to feel offended that Kerrigan had left out this particular scene when he recounted his tale—perhaps it was too recent, too raw—in the end, he just couldn't bring himself to believe this version of the story. He would soon have no other choice, though, because a few days later, Fordington-Lewthwaite produced some irrefutable evidence to support his cause: the weapon that Kerrigan had fired into Collins's head, a fully executed letter of confession that Kerrigan seemed to have signed of his own volition, and a few of the boatswain's personal effects which, having been found in a chest of drawers in Kerrigan's cabin, proved that the captain was not only a murderer but a thief as well. And while Arledge might have questioned the authenticity of the evidence—it could have, after all, been produced and planted by Fordington-Lewthwaite himself—he also knew that the pompous de facto captain, while an ambitious, loathsome fiend to the core, would never have dared enter the realm of illegality, and lacked in any case the imagination necessary to weave such complex and intricate tales.

This startling new bit of news stunned the expeditioners enough to draw them out of their self-absorbed gloom, and at first they categorically refused to accept Fordington-Lewthwaite's revelation. When Arledge killed Léonide Meffre, the other passengers were all still quite exhausted and recovering from the shock of Kerrigan's outburst on deck, and so none of them—with the exception of Miss Bonington—had really been able to muster the appropriate indignation at what Arledge had done—in very cold blood, it should be noted. But when they learned that Kerrigan had indeed killed Eugene Collins—a man that the majority of them scarcely remembered—they exploded and, fuelled by their newly liberated fury, dredged up the matter of the French poet's death, and decided that it was just one more example of how violence and impunity had taken over their diabolical boat, and Arledge suffered the consequences of this. Miss Cook, Mr. Littlefield, and Mr. Beauvais abruptly stopped speaking to him. Florence Bonington, feeling vindicated now that her fellow passengers had finally validated her grievances after ignoring them for so long, actually insulted Arledge as they ate lunch one day. The Handls, who had already been acting oddly for the entire trip, did not step in to defend Arledge. And Hugh Everett Bayham's attitude toward Arledge only grew icier than before. Only Lederer Tourneur—a gentleman who was a bit tiresome to be with but no doubt a fair and just man—did not turn on Arledge, though he certainly didn't go so far as to stand up to the other passengers about it; he simply maintained a dignified but passive position. In retrospect, it seems clear that the other passengers grew so suddenly and intensely hostile toward Victor Arledge not just because he had challenged Léonide Meffre to a duel and won, but because everyone knew that Arledge was Kerrigan's only friend, and since the true culprit of all the Tallahassee's misfortunes was locked up in his cabin and beyond their reach, the passengers heaped all their anger and frustrations on the English novelist, the man closest to Kerrigan, turning him into the redeemer of all the suffering they had endured. Arledge did his best to remain as arrogant and haughty as he knew how, and he also tried to make himself as invisible as he could: no longer did he lay out on the lounge chairs deep in thought, or while away the afternoons strolling on deck, and instead of dining with the other passengers, he had his lunch served to him in his cabin and emerged to eat dinner at the very latest hour, when only the last stragglers left in the dining room were the night owls and sometime gamblers. He spent entire days locked up in his cabin, scrawling random phrases and sentences that, unfortunately, are no longer in my possession. In the end, however, the scorn of his fellow passengers was not what really destroyed Victor

Arledge. It seems that the English novelist was still tormented by his very pressing need to know more about Hugh Everett Bayham's adventure in Scotland, to learn the names of the sisters who lived on the second floor of that mansion, to resolve the mystery of the young woman who seduced him. At the same time he also realized that, for a variety of different reasons, his chances of one day actually possessing such information were growing exponentially smaller as the days went by. His relationship with the gentleman pianist, which had been strained at the beginning, improved slightly over time only to grow icy again, and was now nonexistent. The few times they crossed paths in the halls or on the upper deck, Hugh Everett Bayham maintained his gentlemanly reputation by acknowledging Arledge's presence with a simple nod of the head, and whenever Arledge appeared in any of the sailboat's various salons or lounges, he and the other passengers very pointedly withdrew to another location. Most probably, had Victor Arledge chosen that other alternative following the death of Léonide Meffre—that night of his sad deliberation—he would have had Fordington-Lewthwaite call at Oran or Mostaganem so that he could abandon the *Tallahassee* for good. But his curiosity—buoyed by a kind of never-ending optimism—and his total lack of judgment (and other abilities) kept him from making that decision, which forced him to remain with the expedition until the very end.

However, as is so often the case when a man finds himself enduring the most humiliating of circumstances, the worst was yet to come: not long afterward, Kerrigan managed to escape his cabin, a turn of events that very unexpectedly aggravated Victor Arledge's predicament.

One morning, two of the thugs that Fordington-Lewthwaite had placed in charge of guarding and feeding the captain were preparing to deliver Kerrigan his meager breakfast (and very possibly the daily thrashing that, according to some reports, Fordington-Lewthwaite also ordered them to administer) when they discovered that Kerrigan had somehow managed to force open his door unbeknownst to his night watchmen—a pair of burly sailors who regularly abandoned their post to toss back scotches and kick up their heels with their crewmates, and who had a tendency to fall asleep at the drop of a hat—and make it off the sailboat thanks to their negligence. The crew quickly realized that one of the smaller dinghies was missing and came to the rapid conclusion that Kerrigan had used it to make his escape. Upon hearing the news, Fordington-Lewthwaite responded with loud words and curses, and promised that he himself would make sure that the guilty parties were punished accordingly. But that wasn't all: indignant and irate beyond all proportions, he stormed over to Arledge's cabin, broke the door down with a single blow, and burst into—to simply say "abruptly entered" would be an understatement—the private quarters of the English novelist, who had just barely gotten dressed and now glared at Fordington-Lewthwaite with eyes that were as icy as a mountain gale.

"How did he do it?" Fordington-Lewthwaite shouted. "How did he do it? Answer me!"

Arledge looked him up and down, and then replied, "I have no idea what you are talking about, but I must warn you that it will be no easy task to repair that door. You would be wise to go and advise one of your underlings to get started on it."

Fordington-Lewthwaite, his eyes sparkling with the gleam of ill-contained fury, went over to Arledge and grabbed him by the lapels of the jacket he had just put on. By now, a few passengers had gathered at the spot where the door had been toppled, and contemplated the scene from there.

"I asked you a question, Mr. Arledge, and I demand an answer! How did he get that door open? Was it you? Yes, of course it was!"

Arledge, though he had grown quite despondent as the result of his ostracism, had somehow hung on to his valor. Without flinching, he looked Fordington-Lewthwaite straight in the eye and said, "My dear friend, I would like to advise you to remove your hands from my lapel if you do not wish to find yourself in the same situation as Léonide Meffre, who was far more sensible a man than you."

Fordington-Lewthwaite, somewhat mollified by Victor Arledge's glacial tone of voice, and perhaps by the memory of Meffre's body falling into the sea, regained his composure, shrugged, and removed his hands from Arledge's lapels. Now, with far less conviction than before, he repeated his question: "Did you help him escape?"

Arledge straightened out his suit and responded, "I still have no idea what you are talking about, sir."

"Don't try to fool me, Arledge, you know exactly what I'm talking about. Kerrigan's gone."

Arledge's tone of voice grew even harder and more disdainful.

"You, my dear sailor," he said, "are so dense that you couldn't possibly tell whether I was lying or telling the truth, and for that reason I do not reproach you for your accusations. But you are very wrong. I would have loved to have helped Kerrigan escape, but I did not. Believe me, I am terribly sorry I couldn't. I should have thought of it but I didn't."

At this, Fordington-Lewthwaite lost control of himself. He spun around to face the ever-growing crowd that had gathered at the door to the cabin, and shouted, "Did you hear that? Did you hear that loud and clear? He just admitted that he was the one who helped Kerrigan escape!"

Lederer Tourneur stepped in at this point.

"Don't be ridiculous, Fordington-Lewthwaite. We all heard what Arledge said."

Fordington-Lewthwaite spun back around to face Arledge and asked him, "You just admitted that you would have been delighted to have helped Kerrigan escape, did you not?"

"That's right."

"How do we know, then, that you didn't do it?"

"Such an idiotic question does not deserve an answer," replied Arledge.

Fordington-Lewthwaite began to walk toward the threshold, and said, "Wonham! Come in here with two of your men and arrest this subject immediately!"

A few sailors, trailing behind the aforementioned Wonham, appeared before Fordington-Lewthwaite, but just then Lederer Tourneur intervened again, saying, "Listen to me, Fordington-Lewthwaite. You are taking things too far. Do not start abusing your power, for it is not going to be yours much longer. You know full well that Captain Seebohm has almost completely recovered from his injuries, and I am perfectly willing to offer my version of the facts to whomever I must. What you are doing is illegal, and mark my words, if you arrest Mr. Arledge I will bring you to court myself on more than a few charges the minute we reach a port under British jurisdiction."

At that moment, the dream of becoming captain and commander of his very own ship must have flashed through Fordington-Lewthwaite's mind, and after Tourneur spoke his piece, in a voice so low that the other passengers only heard the slightest murmur, he seemed to calm down somewhat and replied: "All right. But I will be keeping my eye on him, you can't stop me from doing that. I am responsible, if only temporarily, for this ship, and there have been far too many calamities aboard it already. I will not permit this individual to commit another crime. He is cut from the same cloth as Kerrigan, which means he is a very dangerous man."

"I think you are wrong about that, but if that is how you feel, you may keep a watch on him. I won't stop you from doing so. But I will not sit back and allow you to arrest a man without any evidence that he has committed a crime. And let me warn you,

I will not accept any proof that Mr. Arledge helped Kerrigan escape unless it can be verified as authentic."

Fordington-Lewthwaite's face grew somber.

"I would never do such a thing, Mr. Tourneur," he said, in a conciliatory tone. "I am truly sorry for what has happened. I was not in control of my actions. Please accept my apology."

"The person you should be apologizing to is Mr. Arledge, Fordington-Lewthwaite, not me."

Fordington-Lewthwaite looked at Arledge, who had settled into an easy chair and was now smoking a cigarette, and replied: "That, sir, is asking too much."

With that, he began issuing orders as he and his men softly retreated.

Unfortunately, the die had been cast. Lederer Tourneur, despite his good intentions, had made a very grave mistake: first, he had spoken to Fordington-Lewthwaite in very hushed tones, and afterward he did not tell his travel companions what they had discussed. Tourneur was the kind of man for whom acting as fairly and decently as he knew how was its own reward; he had no need for public recognition. His was a personal, private sort of satisfaction: to feel at peace with himself, not anyone else, was the important thing to him. And this very guileless notion—not his admiration of Arledge—was what inspired him to intervene on behalf of the novelist. Tourneur was glad to see Wonham and his men withdraw, but this effectively etched Fordington-Lewthwaite's accusations and Victor Arledge's impertinent replies in the memory of the passengers, who after all had only been privy to those acrimonious words. Arledge had not even bothered to defend himself, maintaining a very unsympathetic attitude throughout, according to the other passengers. And given that they were already predisposed to think ill of him, they now simply took for granted that Fordington-Lewthwaite had been right and that his accusations had been justified. Once again, Victor Arledge was made to endure the consequences of Captain Kerrigan's obstreperous, headstrong character, which so unwittingly caused him a great deal of trouble and brought on much of the torment that he would endure during the last years of his life.

By the time the *Tallahassee* was sailing through Moroccan waters, and the passengers who were planning to disembark at Tangiers emerged from their personal hideouts to chat enthusiastically on deck about the expedition's imminent end, Victor Arledge, following three bitter days of reclusion, came out of his cabin and walked toward the lounge chairs on the upper deck, which was deserted as it always was. He sat down in one of the chairs, and after fifteen tension-filled minutes during which he just gazed out at the horizon, he stood up and looked around for a crew member. After a few moments he located a very young man who was no doubt a cabin boy, walked over to him, handed him a note, and told him to deliver it personally to Hugh Everett Bayham. The cabin boy promised to fulfill the order immediately, and Arledge returned to the lounge chairs, where he sat back down and smoked vast quantities of cigarettes for the following forty-five minutes or so, until he heard footsteps approaching, at which point he stood up. It was Lederer and Marjorie Tourneur: veritably giddy now that they would soon be disembarking at Tangiers and would never have to lay eyes on the *Tallahassee* again, they were enjoying a brief stroll on deck, arm in arm. When they spied Arledge, they smiled, shook his hand warmly, and sat down next to him. Arledge, it seems, appeared nervous and uncomfortable during the conversation.

"How are you?" asked Tourneur. "You haven't been out in days."

"Fine, Mr. Tourneur, just fine," Arledge replied. "You certainly know, perhaps better than anyone else, that my presence is not exactly appreciated on the *Tallahassee* these days."

The Tourneurs were in very good spirits, and Lederer gave

him a rather inappropriate slap on the back and replied: "Don't get soft now, Arledge. Remember, you still have quite a while ahead of you on this boat. If you keep up like this, you won't be able to make it through the rest of your journey."

"Well, surely the two of you must have heard the latest news. In all probability the *Tallahassee* will not make it all the way to Antarctica. Fordington-Lewthwaite had a meeting with the other officers and gave them a detailed report on the situation. It would be absolute folly to undertake such an endeavor given the state of things. It would be madness."

"I didn't hear a thing," said Tourneur. "And I have to wonder how you could have possibly heard that kind of information given that you are so very isolated from the social life on board."

"Well, as you know, two massive men have been standing guard over the door to my miserable cabin. Last night I heard them talking. I thought the news was common knowledge and that I was, in fact, the last to hear of it. You see, Captain Seebohm is almost entirely recovered, but he is still far too weak to endure heaven knows how many more weeks on the Atlantic. And Kerrigan… well, we all know what has become of the man who organized this insane expedition. Fordington-Lewthwaite hasn't the experience necessary to act as their substitute for such a long period of time, and he hasn't the rank, either. The majority of the Manchurian ponies have perished, and I highly doubt we would even be able to locate dogs that could replace them in Tangiers. The passengers are all terribly tired. I do believe they regret having demanded we take this initial leisure cruise, and some of them have already suggested that we give up the expedition altogether and disembark at Tangiers, all of us, or else set sail for Marseilles so that we may all return home from there. The crew, if tacitly, has sided with this group—in fact, the scientists are the only ones who insist that we continue on to the South Pole. If we cancel the trip now, they say, we will have wasted their very valuable time, and they are threatening to demand a very steep compensation if the *Tallahassee* goes no farther than Tangiers. Then again, as you know, since we are the ones who financed the project in the first place, one can assume that we have the last word about what is to be done. In all probability we will disembark at Tangiers, I think."

Lederer Tourneur sighed, ran his hand over his blond hair, and asked: "What do you make of this, Arledge?"

"Well, as you can imagine, I would be thrilled, Mr. Tourneur. Nothing appeals to me more than waking up once again in my comfortable flat on the Rue Buffault or spending a nice long stretch of time in the countryside. I do believe that is what I miss most of all: peace, order, tranquility. Though we do have to wait to see what Captain Seebohm has to say, thanks to those bloody scientists, I will anxiously await the moment we arrive at Tangiers. I feel certain that my journey will end there."

"But what if, on a whim, he decides to sail on to Antarctica?" Marjorie Tourneur queried.

"Even so," Arledge replied, "the bit of curiosity that compelled me to join this expedition is about to be satisfied." Somewhat ruffled, he turned to face the other direction.

"Yes, I can imagine. This cruise has not been terribly pleasant for you, has it? Things have gotten far out of hand, for no good reason, and you have certainly paid the price. Especially with Lambert Littlefield and Miss Cook, most of all—their behavior has been truly exasperating."

"Yes, I know," replied Arledge, grateful for Mrs. Tourneur's sympathies. "But it doesn't matter much at this point. Perhaps my plans would have been successful had it not been for them and Miss Bonington, but those plans no longer depend on them. On the other hand, I do believe I made a mistake by accepting Mr. Meffre's challenge, and for that reason alone I do fear that I must bear some of the responsibility for all that has happened."

Lederer Tourneur, incensed by this, suddenly spoke up: "You had no choice but to accept the challenge, Arledge. Don't be ridiculous. The duel was perfectly legitimate, and nobody can very well blame you for being a good shot. We are all sorry that Meffre is dead, just as we would have been sorry had you died instead, but he was the one who made the mistake by challenging you when he knew perfectly well that the odds were on your side. What else could you have possibly done? We are all gentlemen here, are we not?"

Arledge was nervous, he was anxious, and he was also profoundly exhausted. He paused for a few moments, and then, very slowly, said, "Yes, Mr. Tourneur, we are all gentlemen. Including Captain Kerrigan."

Lederer Tourneur and his wife, somewhat perplexed by Arledge's odd mood as well as his allusions to plans and interests they knew nothing of, stood up and bid him farewell with broad smiles as they resumed their stroll along the deck.

Now, the story I am about to tell you is something I learned from Lederer Tourneur's nephew. He heard it from his late uncle, who described it as one of the most deplorable tales he had ever heard, condemning Victor Arledge's behavior and calling it an outright disgrace to the man's dignity. If only Lederer Tourneur been a bit less adamant, a bit less of a gentleman, we might have finally learned the reasons for Arledge's subsequent disappearance and death. We would have had a definitive answer to this enigma instead of the vague assumptions and dubious conclusions that we have been forced to draw.

As I mentioned before, the Tourneurs had resumed their stroll. But just as they began walking, Hugh Everett Bayham suddenly appeared at the lounge chairs on the upper deck, sending a terse, curt nod of the head in the direction of the short-story writer and his wife, who couldn't help but notice that Bayham's face was unusually red. Alarmed about what might come to pass, they stood where they were for three whole minutes before they finally realized the reason for his wrath, and just as they saw Bayham confront Victor Arledge head-on, they retreated from the scene post-haste. Arledge sucked in his breath, almost as if he were afraid that Bayham might strike him yet willing to endure the blow none-theless, but the pianist merely brandished the note Arledge had sent him via the cabin boy, and as he waved the sheet of paper in the air in front of Arledge, he barked: "What is the meaning of this message, sir?"

Arledge, no doubt inhibited by the presence of the Tourneurs, hesitated a moment, but then nodded to indicate that he intended to respond, which he then did: "It means exactly what it says. I suppose you have read it. But I scarcely think it is anything to get quite so excited over."

Bayham unfolded the paper and read aloud: "My dear Mr. Bayham: I most solicitously ask you to join me by the lounge chairs on the upper deck as soon as you are available, for I wish to speak with you about a subject of extreme importance (to me, at the very least): your recent visit to Scotland. I fervently hope that you will not find any reason to refuse me. Please believe me when I say I would never make such a request if it were not of the most vital importance to me, as I mentioned before. Yours truly, Victor Arledge."

The novelist couldn't help but blush as he heard his words read aloud, and said, "I hardly think it necessary to read that in public, Mr. Bayham. But now that you have done so, I assume that every-one here would agree that the letter is quite clear even if the style might leave something to be desired."

"The note is far too clear, Mr. Arledge, and that is why I find it so startling. I thought we had resolved this matter once and for all in Alexandria."

"It may have been resolved for you, Mr. Bayham, but not for me. This is a matter that continues to pique my interest in the most vexing way."

"Oh, why?"

"I wouldn't know how to explain it, and even if I did I doubt I could express it very well. You would simply never understand. Let us just say that it offered the shadow of an idea for a new novel. Perhaps you will find that response satisfactory, Mr. Bayham."

"I simply don't understand it. I would never have imagined that your curiosity went so deep, and I must say that it is a most unpleasant surprise."

"It goes very deep, Mr. Bayham, very deep indeed," Arledge acknowledged.

"During that uncomfortable exchange in Alexandria," the pianist went on, "I was taken aback by you, and your insistence, but after our little conversation on the way back to the port that afternoon, I had assumed that we had put it all behind us. Now, however, I see that you have continued thinking about all this ever since then, like a cow chewing her cud. You are a very stubborn man."

At that point Arledge still hadn't lost his mild manner or sense of humor.

"Though your bovine allusion does not flatter me, Mr. Bayham, I must admit that it is the most appropriate of any you might have used, and I congratulate you for that."

"This is no time for jokes, Arledge. I repeat my question: what is the meaning of this message?"

"It means," responded Arledge, slightly impatient, "that I wish you would tell me the truth about what happened to you that night in Scotland after you were kidnapped by three men in a carriage that you entered voluntarily after performing, quite brilliantly, at a piano concert, the program of which consisted of works by Brahms and Clementi."

At first Bayham could only stare at Arledge, dumbfounded. Then he cried out, "Damn you! That carriage never existed."

Victor Arledge's face crumpled. Without missing a beat, he grabbed Bayham by the tail of his jacket and, still seated, pulled him close.

"What do you mean 'that carriage never existed'?" he demanded, repeating Bayham's words. "What is that supposed to mean?"

Hugh Everett Bayham suddenly realized that he had said too much. With a violent movement, he extricated himself from Arledge's grip and said: "I did not mean a thing by it. Leave me alone already."

Arledge rose up from his chair and grabbed him again, this time by the lapels of his jacket. In what came out sounding like both a plea and a demand, he cried out, "No! You must tell me! Now! Right now, you must tell me everything!"

Bayham once again extricated himself from Arledge's tight grip, and replied: "I shall not tell you anything, Mr. Arledge. I have no need. These are private matters that concern me and only me. For the last time, please forget you ever heard anything."

Arledge, it seems, had lost control of himself by then. I don't dare repeat his vehement pleas here, but according to Lederer Tourneur's nephew, they were quite embarrassing indeed. He begged Bayham tirelessly, shamelessly, grabbing him again and again, and Bayham just kept on wiggling away again and again. At one point, Arledge even broke down and sobbed. Without a doubt, Lederer Tourneur, such a sober, reserved gentleman, was terribly affected by the scene and found it utterly distasteful. When he could no longer bear to witness any more of this spectacle, he took his wife's arm, and the two of them left without saying another word. As they walked away, however, he did hear the voice of Hugh Everett Bayham, who, upon seeing Arledge in a state of such profound desperation, and more than anything to keep him from doing something truly insane, finally agreed to tell him what had really happened that night in Scotland—but this, of course, was a matter that did not hold the slightest bit of meaning or interest for Lederer Tourneur.

To date, nobody has ever been able to ascertain exactly what happened to Hugh Everett Bayham that night in Scotland, though we may be quite certain that whatever it was, Victor Arledge found it exceedingly underwhelming. Perhaps it was all a lie, and the carriage was but one of many things that never existed, as he put it; perhaps Bayham made it all up to justify an unjustifiable absence, perhaps it was a simple ruse to arouse the jealousy of his wife, Margaret Holloway, and thereby precipitate their separation; or perhaps the carriage was the only thing that "never existed" and the story in fact ended as it had in Esmond Handl's initial letter to Arledge. We will never know the answer to these questions—I, at the very least, have been unable to reach any real sort of conclusion. But then sometimes I just tell myself that it isn't so important after all and that in the end, no matter what really happened, it is not a story that is really worth repeating.

The following morning Victor Arledge emerged from his cabin at a very early hour, looking far better than he had in several days, and his face literally radiated serenity. He then walked toward the dining room and proceeded to eat breakfast in the company of his fellow passengers who, though not particularly cordial, were more or less courteous—inspired, perhaps, by the general feeling of glee that had come over them during those last few days on board. Arledge devoted the rest of his day to the same activities that he had often enjoyed before the death of Léonide Meffre had changed things, and spoke with no one other than Esmond and Clara Handl. But he no longer made any effort, as he had been doing previously, to avoid the reproachful gazes and whispers of whatever expeditioners were in his immediate vicinity. From this point onward until the end of the voyage, there were no more sudden changes in his behavior: his attitude was timidly, tentatively amiable, and it seems that he even made an attempt to patch things up with some of the other passengers, most specifically Miss Cook, Lambert Littlefield, and Mr. Beauvais. And then, in an act of total abnegation, he asked Mr. Bayham and Mr. Bonington to teach him the rudiments of certain card games, and spent an entire evening in their company, learning how to determine the values of this card and that.

Captain Eustace Seebohm, for his part, made a full recovery from the wounds he sustained during Kerrigan's attack and was soon strong enough to reassume the command of the ship, and though this did serve as a rather unpleasant reminder of all the terrible things that had come to pass because of one Captain Joseph Dunhill Kerrigan, the passengers of the *Tallahassee* were far too content to be bothered and in no way sharpened their invective against Victor Arledge. They simply avoided bringing up certain unpleasant topics of conversation and pointedly made sure that they didn't spend too much time in the company of the novelist. Fordington-Lewthwaite assumed his previous position in the boat's pecking order, without a word of praise from his superior, who felt that his subordinate had inappropriately interfered with the private affairs of the passengers and that in his eagerness to rectify certain matters, Fordington-Lewthwaite had only succeeded in generating a whole new spate of problems that had created a very unpleasant atmosphere of fear and anxiety on board the sailboat.

It soon became clear that Tangiers would be the final destination of the *Tallahassee,* though the decision was made not by Captain Seebohm but rather by certain events that soon unfolded before their eyes. The *Tallahassee* was cruising along the Moroccan coastline close to the Algerian border when, out of nowhere, shots rang out in the air; they seemed to be coming from the direction of the shore. The passengers and crew fell to the deck, but the gunfire continued. The vessel's wooden frame suddenly began splintering off into tiny pieces, and the lifeboats, which were very visibly hanging by thick ropes above the deck, were soon riddled with bullets. Even after peering into his binoculars Captain Seebohm was unable to discern anything, not even the kind of clothing worn by their assailants, whom he believed had sought cover behind a massive sand dune. For several minutes, as a small number of brave sailors obeyed his orders to climb up to the tip of the main mast to ascertain the identity of the men firing at them, Seebohm did not know whether to head toward land and confront the attackers with his amateur crew—amateurs, at least, in the matter of combat and vessel defense—or turn toward the open sea until they were beyond the reach of the bullets presently being fired at them. The sailors climbed back down and informed the captain that from the top of the main mast they had not been able to see a single man, much less anyone firing away with a repeating rifle, which seemed to be the attackers' weapon of choice, judging by the volume of bullets that had peppered the boat. The passengers, however, most of whom had been on deck when the gunfire commenced and hadn't had the time to run inside to their cabins, were in a state of total panic, and Seebohm quickly abandoned the idea of facing up to their invisible enemy. As he issued the corresponding orders to his crew, the boat began to retreat from the shoreline. But as soon as the gunfire came to a halt and they seemed to be out of danger's way, the expeditioners jumped to their feet, wondering who on earth could have opened fire like that against them, and as they shook the dust from their suits and dresses and checked for broken bones, they all realized that the shower of bullets that had made a pock-marked mess of the *Tallahassee*'s hull had been so heavy that it would be a minor miracle if they arrived at Tangiers in one piece.

Now, just to make sure that Clara Handl's one and only question did not go unanswered—it should be noted that the attackers were none other than Raisuli, the rebel, and his group of insurgents.

BOOK SEVEN

Voyage *Along the Horizon* had come to an end. Mr. Holden Branshaw shut the book with a resounding clap and, without a word, got up from the easy chair he had occupied for almost three hours, walked over to one of the bookshelves, and very carefully placed the book back in its original place, next to an excellent edition of George du Maurier's complete works. He then poured a glass of Italian wine and offered it to me, though I declined, preferring to savor one of my imported Turkish cigarettes. At that, he sat back down in his chair and, with a sigh of tremendous fatigue, took a sip of the wine. When he noticed me digging through my pockets for a match, he quickly produced a lighter and very politely lit my cigarette. At that point, I stood up, and as I exhaled a few deep puffs of smoke, I took a little stroll around the room, occasionally stopping to admire some of the rare volumes in his book collection or one of the ceramic pieces sitting upon the mantel. Aside from the few words Branshaw uttered when he asked me if I would care for a glass of wine or some other beverage, and my own terse reply, it was as if neither of us dared to speak; as if neither of us could bring ourselves

to make even the slightest reference to the novel that we had just
finished reading. Perhaps because he was a very methodical man,
or perhaps because he felt the manuscript had been out of its
proper place for far too much time already, Branshaw had rushed
to place it back in its spot on the bookshelf, effectively forcing the
disappearance of the obvious object of our attention and conversation. And though my gaze insistently wandered back to the
bookshelf that held the complete illustrated works of George du
Maurier, distressed that the novel written by Mr. Branshaw's friend
was now out of my sight and reach, I had the distinct feeling that
I would be unable to speak about the novel at all unless the volume was taken off the shelf and once again made an integral part
of Mr. Branshaw's figure. With this in mind, I summoned my
courage and asked him if I might take a look at it, but my host
replied, with a faint smile, that he thought it was time to give the
book a bit of a rest, and that he would rather we left it where it
was if I didn't mind. Naturally, I replied that I understood perfectly,
even though I did think he was being a bit ridiculous given that it
was just a simple manuscript. After that I fell silent, preferring to
study Mr. Branshaw instead: I noticed that as he took tiny sips of
Italian wine, he did not seem to be waiting for me to express any
kind of opinion, as he had at other moments, as when we had finished the first part of *Voyage Along the Horizon*. This time around,
he paid no attention to me whatsoever and just stared intently at
the rug beneath his feet with a vaguely disenchanted look on his
face. He also seemed quite tired, but I didn't find that nearly as
surprising—after all, he had been reading aloud for several
hours—as the disgruntled expression on his face and his very obvious lack of interest in my opinion of the book.

I was offended by this, and just as I was about to tell him that
I thought his late friend's novel was in fact excellent, and that it
was quite sad that such a significant author had died such a pre-
mature death, Holden Branshaw emerged from his personal trance

and spoke up before I could, in a tone of voice that was rather poignant: "May I tell you something? I've just realized that my friend's novel isn't nearly as good as I thought it was."

I was taken aback by this, and quickly began defending the novel, but Branshaw just shook his head from side to side as if to tell me he had no need for sympathetic lies. Then he said, "I have read this novel ten times over in the silence of my little room, and I have always thought it a minor masterpiece that was far superior to anything else written in our time. It wasn't that I found it so terribly original, astounding, brilliant, or inimitable, but I was terribly fond of it, really fascinated by Victor Arledge's story, and for a book of such sober style, I did feel that it was quite exceptional. But as I said before, this opinion was formed in the silence of my room. Ever since my friend died, I have felt that his book absolutely had to be published; once in the hands of the public, I thought, this book would finally place Edward among the great novelists of his time, but at the same time I must admit that I had never associated *Voyage Along the Horizon* with anyone but myself and the four walls of my office. What I mean is that I never considered the effect it might have on other people, other readers—without truly thinking about it, I always assumed that other people would naturally share my opinion. But I was wrong to assume such a thing, I'm afraid, and I have only realized it just now, as I read the second part aloud to you. My friend's novel is, unfortunately, mediocre. It reveals only the literary pretensions of an eager young writer. Well, I don't know—perhaps I shouldn't be quite so harsh, perhaps I am allowing my anger to get the best of me. And it may even be possible that *Voyage Along the Horizon* is in fact a very respectable novel, but then what is 'respectable' compared to the destiny I had envisioned for it? A terrible disappointment, I can assure you. No, no—please do not interrupt me. I am telling you the truth. My friend's novel should never be published and should never have been read or listened to by anyone other than myself. That way, at least, it might not have lost its charm the way it did for me, and I could have continued to harbor the illusion that one day it might actually get published. But alas, things took a different turn, and perhaps it is better this way. I must confess that as I read you the second part of the novel, I couldn't help but wonder what you thought of it, and more than once I was tempted to stop reading and ask your opinion. Now, however, I have no interest whatsoever in knowing what you think. I am more than satisfied with my own opinion, by imagining your opinion of the novel—in other words, the opinion of someone who never met Edward Ellis, who never knew that Victor Arledge spent the last years of his life hidden away in a country mansion owned by a distant Scottish relative, as the result of a curiosity that turned out to be a tremendous disappointment. And, with this opinion in mind—that is, the opinion of someone who never knew any of this—the novel indeed leaves much to be desired. Perhaps you find my reasoning arbitrary or childish, or feel that it lacks a certain perspective, and that I am simply expressing a momentary disillusion. But that is not the case. I have thought a great deal about it, and I only fear that with more time and more thought, with a more serene, distant, and objective perspective than I am capable of at the moment, my opinion will only grow stronger. For the moment I believe you were right when you at first said you found the story cumbersome—it is irrelevant that you no longer think so; you said it, and the idea took root in my mind—and that Miss Bunnage was wise not to bother joining us today. Yes, Miss Bunnage, despite what she may have said on other occasions, has always seemed to me to be a very intelligent woman."

Mr. Branshaw's speech, though it interested me, was beginning to show signs of growing more and more nostalgic, and of droning on infinitely. On one hand I simply didn't understand the reason for his very sudden disenchantment with the novel by Edward Ellis—at last, I had learned the author's name!—and moreover

I found his reasoning rather puerile and capricious. But what finally compelled me to interrupt him was his reference to Miss Bunnage. I had forgotten about her completely, and as I heard her name and recalled her face, I started to grow alarmed by her absence, and wondered what exactly had become of her. And so I asked him: "Mr. Branshaw, do you have any idea how Mr. Ellis managed to find out so much about the voyage of the *Tallahassee*? The novel is full of such specific details."

Suddenly, Mr. Branshaw seemed to awaken from a deep sleep, and asked me to repeat the question. I obliged, apologizing for having interrupted his thoughts, and he replied, "Well, you should bear in mind that what my friend wrote was a novel, not a historical account. There are many conversations and situations that he invented himself. Nowhere at all is there any proof that things actually happened the way he said they did."

"I wasn't thinking of that, not exactly, Mr. Branshaw," I replied. "I was referring more to his working method, outside of having questioned Lederer Tourneur's nephew."

"Ah," replied Branshaw. "Well, let's see: he interviewed quite a few other people in addition to Lederer Tourneur's nephew, among them Esmond Handl, who died just four years ago. It was Handl who told him about the letter, and some other details as well. And many of the other passengers are still alive, in quite excellent health, as a matter of fact. But the lion's share of the information he uncovered he found in the Scottish mansion that belonged to Arledge's relative, not far from Perth. Victor Arledge left behind some notes about the trip there: a pile of incomprehensible, scattered bits of material that was too insignificant to publish, but Edward, having already gleaned a certain amount of information, understood many of the references in these notes and actually found them useful."

"It seems to me," I said, "that I have noticed a few technical errors here. For example, I believe that the *Tallahassee,* at least according to the novel, took far too long to get from Alexandria to Tangiers."

"I don't doubt it at all. First of all, Edward Ellis knew nothing about navigation. And of course, he died before he was able to correct the novel. But after all, he was writing fiction, and from his point of view this type of error is inadmissible only in an essay or chronicle."

"Right, right," I murmured, and stood up.

"Are you leaving, so soon?" asked Branshaw, rising to his feet as well.

"Yes, sir. I'm sorry, but I do have obligations I must attend to," I replied. "I do appreciate your kindness, Mr. Branshaw, and I hope that we will be able to speak about *Voyage Along the Horizon* on some other occasion, perhaps when the reading is no longer so fresh in your mind, when you have had more time to think about it."

"As you wish, sir, but I must warn you that I have made my decision, and it is irrevocable. The novel will never be published."

I smiled, walked toward the front door, which he opened, and as I offered him my hand to say goodbye, I said: "I do hope that I will be able to change your mind."

Branshaw only smiled again, and replied, "Well, I cannot keep you from hoping, but it will only be in vain. That I can promise you. Goodbye, sir."

"Goodbye, and thank you for everything, Mr. Branshaw."

I walked out, and the front door closed behind me without a sound.

It took me longer than I expected to reach Miss Bunnage's house on Finsbury Road. I was anxious to see her, to find out why she hadn't kept her date that morning at Holden Branshaw's home— I did not, for my part, agree with Branshaw's suspicions in the least—and to see if she might be willing to divulge the many mysteries surrounding *Voyage Along the Horizon*—assuming that she hadn't regretted her promise to me, or considered it moot given that she hadn't attended the second round of Mr. Branshaw's reading. The book had me mesmerized, though my fascination, in reality, went beyond Edward Ellis's writing in and of itself: it was the story and the character of Victor Arledge that had gotten under my skin—Victor Arledge, an author whose name I'd never even heard before the evening of my party. This was why, from the very instant I thought back to Miss Bunnage, I felt unusually excited and agitated, more impatient than ever to learn the details— details that had apparently eluded even Edward Ellis—of the matter that I was now very clearly obsessed with. I had quite a time finding a carriage and driver, and did not reach No. 4 Finsbury Road until a full three-quarters of an hour after leaving Mr. Branshaw's house.

When I reached the front door, I rang the bell but received no response, so I rang again and waited, again in vain. I tried three more times to no avail and finally thought I might have better luck discerning something—anything—if I peered through the windows, but I soon realized that all the shutters except for one on the ground floor were closed. I looked through the one exposed window, but since it was the only path through which any light at all could penetrate, I was unable to see anything—or almost anything outside of the four feet of a chair. I was rather puzzled by all this— why, I wondered, was everything here so quiet, so abandoned? Several possibilities ran through my mind, one of which turned out to be right in the end.

I calmed down a bit after that, but soon enough I began to feel overcome by a terrible wave of fatigue which left me with barely enough strength to do anything but get into another coach and go directly home, which is what I did.

Once home, I drew a bath and ate lunch in the company of my cousin, a lovely, intelligent young lady about twenty-eight years of age, who had recently settled in London and had been patiently waiting for me; I had invited her a week earlier but, of course, I had all but forgotten about our lunch date. Constance— that is her name—could sense that I was distressed and, concerned, asked what was troubling me. Growing more and more nervous by the moment, I suddenly stood up from the table and went to look for Miss Bunnage's telephone number in the directory. I dialed the number but got no response. I was about to call the police when Constance, visibly alarmed by my behavior and my mental state, repeated her question, and so I sat down once again at the table and gave her a general idea of all that had happened over the past two days. She seemed intrigued by the story and concerned about what had become of Miss Bunnage and suggested that we go directly to her house at Finsbury Road and either try to speak to the neighbors to see if they knew anything, or simply sit on the stairs to her front door and wait until she or her maid turned up. I thought this was a fine idea and was relieved that Constance had been the one to suggest it, because I had been thinking the same thing though never would have mentioned it myself for fear it would sound ridiculous and excessive on my part. So I thanked her for thinking of such a wise idea, and we immediately gathered our things to leave. Constance had come in her own coach, and in a matter of minutes we were at the dark green front door to Miss Bunnage's house.

Constance, even more determined than I, went straight to the house next door and rang the bell, but nobody answered there either, so we settled down on the steps in front of 4 Finsbury Road, prepared to stay there as long as was necessary. As it turned out we didn't have to wait long: after no more than ten minutes we watched as three black coaches advanced toward us in single file and then came to a stop in front of the house—an odd sight on that street, which rarely saw much traffic—and a total of twelve people stepped down, among them Miss Bunnage's elderly maid.

My suspicions were confirmed as I noted that everyone wore either black or gray, and their faces were terribly crestfallen. The elderly maid, aided by two men (no doubt the neighbors who hadn't answered the door) walked over to where Constance and I were waiting. The two of us stood up, and I very solemnly asked the maid: "What has happened? Where is Miss Bunnage?" I quickly realized that the maid had not recognized me, and so I added, "Don't you remember me? I ate lunch with Miss Bunnage in her house just yesterday."

The old woman studied my face until she finally seemed to recognize me; she may have been momentarily confused by the presence of Constance.

"We just laid her to rest," she replied, and waved me away so that she could enter the house.

Constance and I quickly moved aside, but before the elderly maid was able to disappear through the door, I asked her if Miss Bunnage had left a message for me, and then I gave her my name. She turned around and shook her head no.

The neighbors then explained to me that Miss Bunnage, who had had a very delicate heart, had suffered a heart attack and died instantly the night before. In her last will and testament she left everything to her elderly maid: the house, the paintings, the furniture, the books, and a bit of money all belonged to her now.

BOOK EIGHT

In the two years that followed, I married my cousin Constance—though I cannot say to what point the events of that afternoon had anything to do with our decision to wed—and I went to live in the United States for professional reasons. Little by little I forgot about Miss Bunnage, Mr. Holden Branshaw (or was it Hordern Bragshawe? I never did find out), and *Voyage Along the Horizon,* but it never fully escaped my mind; every so often, as my sweet and charming wife waited for me in bed as I lingered before going to sleep with some or other book, she would ask me about the things Miss Bunnage had promised to tell me about Edward Ellis's book. And though he is not a very well-known writer in America and his works are not easy to locate there, a few of Victor Arledge's novels somehow managed to find their way to me, very coincidentally, though I found them all quite inferior to *Voyage Along the Horizon,* of which he had been not the author but rather the central character. This, then, made me wonder why Mr. Branshaw's friend had dedicated his life and fortune to learning the motive that could have driven such an unexceptional author to abandon his literary vocation.

Approximately two years after the afternoon we learned of Miss Bunnage's death, my wife was suddenly called back to England to visit her father, who was on his deathbed and wished to see his daughter before he expired. When she returned, sad but happy to be back with me, she handed me a gift: it seems that she had paid a visit to 4 Finsbury Road and had managed to convince Miss Bunnage's elderly maid to sell her a folder filled with papers that had belonged to Miss Bunnage and which had still not been sold to the academics that were interested in her critical essays. I examined the folder with great interest, and among the letters, notes, and commentary, I found four sheets of paper, worn away by time, covered with notes written in the first person, in what looked like a man's handwriting—at the very least I knew it was not that of Miss Bunnage. And so I came to my own conclusions, but I nevertheless remained convinced that she knew far more about *Voyage Along the Horizon* than what was left behind on those four pages.

EIGHT QUESTIONS
FOR JAVIER MARÍAS

What are *Voyage Along the Horizon*'s influences?

When I wrote this novel—I was nineteen when I started it, and twenty-one by the time I finished it—I was without a doubt still tremendously influenced by two authors I had been reading quite exhaustively at the time: Joseph Conrad and Henry James. I don't remember exactly which ones influenced me most directly, but *Heart of Darkness* and *Almayer's Folly* by Conrad, and probably James's stories, were surely among them. These influences, plus that of Conan Doyle (or Conan Doyle via Billy Wilder and his movie *The Private Life of Sherlock Holmes,* one of my favorite movies both then and now) in the part about the kidnapping, are not only evident but very deliberate, and I myself acknowledged this the (few) times I was interviewed when the novel first came out in March 1973 (even though the publication date is 1972). I was influenced by James stylistically but also by the atmosphere of his novels, as well as by his method of using indirect narrators who put the story in the hands of someone else who then, in turn, hands it over to a text, etc. My debt to Conrad, most of all, lies in the seafaring theme, and especially in the episode with the character called Lutz, and Captain Kerrigan in general. I haven't reread this novel in many years, so I am guessing that all of this is not only rather obvious but that the tone must necessarily be somewhat artificial. But that was also my intention when I wrote it.

Who is narrating the book, really, and what does he want from us?

Honestly I have no idea. I'm sorry I can't give you a better answer than that. I suppose, though, that it doesn't really matter; when I wrote it I wasn't very concerned about who was narrating the story in the first place. That element, in fact, may be one of the few distinguishable characteristics of my later novels: they are all narrators who are nobody, in reality, just voices, interpreters, people who lend their voices to others or who simply transmit what they have received (in *All Souls,* for example, a professor; in *The Man of Feeling,* a singer; in *A Heart So White,* an interpreter of languages; in *Tomorrow in the Battle Think of Me,* a ghostwriter; in *Your Face Tomorrow,* an interpreter of people, a spy of sorts). They are all people who, you might say, speak a bit from the outside, and in some sense they are ghostly voices. The ghostliest of them all is the narrator of the story "When I Was Mortal," an actual ghost that has been blessed with the capacity to know everything, cursed by the ability to remember everything, but crippled by his inability to take action, anymore. As for the narrator of *Voyage Along the Horizon,* he wants what, I suppose, every narrator wants: to be followed, to persuade, to be accompanied.

Has your experience as a translator affected the way you look at the translations of your own works? Of your sizable literary output, only a relatively small handful of your books have been translated into English—do you see any pattern

among these books, something predisposing them into English translation?

Yes, of course my previous work as a translator (it has been many years since I have translated anything more than a story or a poem here and there; I no longer translate books) has influenced me, both in terms of my own writing as well as the way I view the translations of my own works into other languages. Well, actually, I can speak only of three of the thirty-four languages into which my books have been translated, those I understand: English, French, and Italian. I think that my books, just like other books all over the world, are improved in translation, and I am almost certain that they must be at their best in languages like Korean, Hindi, or Estonian. In any event, the mysterious thing about all this is that in the languages I understand, I continue to recognize the books as the ones I wrote. I think that there are certain authors who, for lack of a better term, have a "contagious" effect on the translator (I am talking about a good translator, of course) who then comfortably settles into the author's music and reproduces it with extreme and almost miraculous precision. This has nothing to do with whether an author is good or bad; it is simply a strange quality that certain texts possess. In my case, at least, this happened to me, as a translator, with Conrad, Sterne, and Sir Thomas Browne, but it did not happen with Yeats or Isak Dinesen, who are equally extraordinary writers. I have the vague sensation that my books have that "contagious" effect on translators, though I am in no way trying to compare myself with anyone when I say that, of course.

In that sense, thinking about the English language, I do get the feeling that my novels almost sound better in English than in Spanish. I have always been very familiar with the English language, and it is entirely possible that because of this, as a writer, I incorporate certain aspects of the English language into my prose in Spanish, and as such it doesn't sound quite so strange when translated into English. Knowing several languages allows you to yearn for what one language has but the others lack, and sometimes as a writer you do feel tempted to add a little something to your language that it doesn't normally have but that you know is possible.

Do you think there's a difference between great Spanish novels and great American novels? What about the difference between English novels and American novels?

The thing that differentiates the world's great novels is usually the setting, which is a relatively secondary issue. The language in which the novel is written is also somewhat secondary, though important. That's how a translator thinks. I can imagine Proust in Italian, Faulkner in Spanish (in fact, there are more than a few Faulkner disciples in my language: García Márquez, Onetti, and Juan Benet, among others), Dickens in French. Why not? With respect to the American novel, the only problem I see with it is that typically nineteenth-century concept, which is the desire to encompass everything, and you can never encompass everything in a novel. With some exceptions of course, European novelists tend not to be so concerned about that, and perhaps they are more conscious that the shadow zones of the world are limitless in scope, and that the only thing a novel can do is illuminate them a bit, not to see anything in them, but rather just to admire the darkness with more clarity, the apparent contradiction notwithstanding.

Along with the play of narrator, there is also the nested narrative of the book—the story of a man listening to a novel read aloud which itself contains plots within plots, and characters who read letters that tell stories inside stories. The book we hold in our hands, titled *Voyage Along the Horizon,* contains a book titled *Voyage Along the Horizon,*

which tells the story of a voyage that never quite makes it to the horizon. And within all of these, there are the different versions (one might even say, translations) of the stories that each character holds; in terms of meaning, the book in Mr. Branshaw's mind is not the same book heard by the narrator, which is not the same book heard by Miss Bunnage. Aside from being terrific fun to read, to what effect does this metanarrative have? To what extent is the medium the message? How do you see your book, which contains prose stylized in the vein of nineteenth-century writers, fitting in with or reacting against the narratives of actual nineteenth-century novels, which themselves often contained such nested and unreliable narration? If *Voyage Along the Horizon* and *Tristram Shandy* got into a fight, who would win?

If *Voyage Along the Horizon* imitates the nineteenth-century novel, it does so with irony, in a manner that is deliberately tongue-in-cheek, as if even then I already know that certain kinds of things would never have been possible in the twentieth century. Nineteenth-century novelists tended to write in the third person, frequently with omniscient narrators. Nowadays this is more and more difficult to accept. We all know that our knowledge is very limited, even when it comes to our own lives. And we also know that we ourselves could never possibly tell our own stories in their entireties. In *Voyage Along the Horizon,* I think there is a certain awareness of this: of the fact that all stories are fragmentary or fleeting glimpses or, to borrow a phrase from Faulkner, like the experience of looking into the darkness after lighting a match in the middle of a forest or a field. And regarding any kind of match-up between *Tristram Shandy* and my youthful novel, that would be like wondering who would win in a fight between Cassius Clay and a featherweight.

Hand in hand with the nineteenth century–style prose, there is the question of class within the novel: as in a novel by Austen or James, the book is populated by people who don't seem ever to have to work, who are contrasted with people who are forced to struggle very hard to survive. Writers and poets and musicians who are never actually seen doing their work are contrasted with dissolute sailors, exasperated scientists, and insurgents whose causes are cursed not even to be revealed to the upper-class folk. This leads to the class-laden question of taste within the novel, and what is and isn't appropriate to be discussed in public, as well as the question of honor, and what is and isn't a tolerable affront to one's dignity. What about class or the nineteenth-century novelistic style interested you such that you wrote a novel in this mode in 1971? What relevance, in respect to contemporary events, do you see these concerns have? Or do they address more timeless questions?

Insofar as *Voyage Along the Horizon* is something of a parody, I would say that the class differences you mention are treated within the context of parody. For me it was great fun to insert myself into a world that, in 1972 or 1973, was already long obsolete. At the same time, the novel expresses a bit of nostalgia for the writer—the novelist—who was a novelist and nothing more, someone who did not feel obligated to express opinions about political and social issues. Nowadays, those of us who are writers spend a lot of time expressing our opinions about almost anything that happens anywhere in the world. At least in Europe this is true. We are constantly being asked to take a "position," or to demonstrate our solidarity with some cause or disaster or problem. For my part I have always made an effort to distinguish between the novelist and the citizen. As a citizen, I have an opinion about far too many things; for the past eleven years I have been writing a column every Sunday about topics of (generally but not necessarily) current interest, and in this sense I feel very much a part of the world, and quite obligated to become involved in what is happening around me.[1] As a novelist, however, I am not a citizen. In that area, I try to steer clear of judgments, moral codes, and, of course, morals at the end of the story. The "artistic" characters in *Voyage Along The Horizon,* I suppose, are precisely that: they are not citizens.

With the benefit of hindsight, do you see anything in the book that foreshadows career-long concerns in your literary output, or anything that seems to you to be dated in terms of your style? Is there anything about the book that surprises you almost thirty-five years later?

One thing I know is that today I would never write a novel anything like *Voyage Along the Horizon.* Perhaps a short story, given that short stories (a tradition completely separate from that of the novel, though both are narrative forms of expression) permit the genre and the subgenre to a greater degree. That is how it is for me, at least. I do think, however, that *Voyage Along the Horizon* does have a way of foreshadowing what I mentioned before, the narrative voice that in reality is just that: a voice completely bereft of corporality. And it also may be the first novel in which I turned the question of doubt and indecision into part of the narrative method and the story itself. What I don't think, however, is that *Voyage Along the Horizon* is a novel that is "out of style," and I know that is saying a lot. But either it already was out of style in 1972 or it never will be. My first two novels (that is, this one and *Los Dominios del Lobo* [*The Dominions of the Wolf*] my first, published

---

[1] English translations of Marías's column, "La Zona Fantasma," appeared monthly in the *Believer* magazine between February 2005 and March 2006.

when I was nineteen, in 1971) possess what I think are various advantages in that (*a*) they were not at all autobiographical; (*b*) they were not "experimental," as was the trend with novels in those days; (*c*) they were not "antinarratives," another trend back then; (*d*) they were not set in Spain; (*e*) they were not set in the same era in which they were written; and (*f*) they had no particular "message," neither ideological nor political nor any other kind. And so if they are, in fact, novels that are still pleasant to read (I'm not one to be the judge of that), these factors may help to make them somewhat atemporal. And that which is atemporal, we all know, ages the least.

What would you tell readers who don't know what to make of the ending?

That the end of a novel isn't usually very important. In fact, people never seem to remember the endings of novels (most especially crime novels—that's what makes them so re-readable) and movies (especially, once again, thrillers and whodunits). Conclusions and final explanations are often the most irrelevant— and disappointing—parts of a novel. What counts the most—and what we remember the most—is the atmosphere, the style, the path, the journey, and the world in which we have immersed ourselves for a few hours or a few days while reading a novel or watching a movie. What matters, then, is the journey along the horizon—in other words, the journey that never ends.

Javier Marías was born in Madrid in 1951. English-language trans-
lations of his books include the novels *All Souls*, *A Heart So White*,
Tomorrow in the Battle Think On Me, *Dark Back of Time*, *Your Face
Tomorrow*, and *The Man of Feeling;* the short-story collection *When
I Was Mortal;* and a collection of mini-biographies of writers,
Written Lives. He won the 1997 International IMPAC Dublin
Literary Award.